THE CHALLENGE

Miriam's eyes gleamed in the darkness. It seemed to her a devil perhaps might be whispering the suggestion. A daring like none she had ever felt before came to her. She would do it. Claude should see her in the same way in which he saw Mrs. Sylvester. He should see that his wife's neck was as white and her arms as well rounded as those of her adversary. For once she would appear as did others. If she was to die fighting, and she felt it was near the end of the battle now, whatever the result, she would die brilliantly. Any scruples she might have had before had fled. What were scruples at such a time? If it was this that Claude admired he should see that his wife could be as beautiful as any. She would die leaving him with the pain of regret in his heart.

Bantam Books by Grace Livingston Hill
Ask your bookseller for the books you have missed

According to the Pattern

GRACE LIVINGSTON HILL

BANTAM BOOKS

TORONTO • NEW YORK • LONDON • SYDNEY • AUCKLAND

This edition contains the complete text
of the original hardcover edition.
NOT ONE WORD HAS BEEN OMITTED.

ACCORDING TO THE PATTERN

A Bantam Book / published by arrangement with
The Estate

PRINTING HISTORY

Originally published: Philadelphia: Griffith and Rowland Press, 1903

Bantam edition / September 1985
5 printings through January 1988

ISBN 0-553-27421-X

Published simultaneously in the United States and Canada

Bantam Books are published by Bantam Books, a division of Bantam
Doubleday Dell Publishing Group, Inc. Its trademark, consisting of the
words "Bantam Books" and the portrayal of a rooster, is Registered in
U.S. Patent and Trademark Office and in other countries. Marca
Registrada. Bantam Books, 666 Fifth Avenue, New York, New York 10103.

PRINTED IN THE UNITED STATES OF AMERICA

O   14   13   12   11   10   9   8   7   6   5

CONTENTS

•

*According to the
Pattern*

CHAPTER 1

·

A Fallen Idol

Mrs. Claude Winthrop sat in her pretty sitting room alone under the lamplight making buttonholes. Her eyes were swimming in stinging tears that she would not for the world let fall. She felt as if a new law of attraction held them there to blind and torture her. She could not let them fall, for no more were left; they were burned up by the emotions that were raging in her soul, and if these tears were gone her eyeballs would surely scorch the lids. She was exercising strong control over her lips that longed to open in a groan that should increase until it reached a shriek that all the world could hear.

Her fingers flew with nervous haste, setting the needle in dainty stitches in the soft white dress for her baby girl. She had not supposed when she fashioned the little garment the day before and laid it aside ready for the finishing that she would think of its wearer to-night in so much agony. Ah, her baby girl, and her boy, and the older sister!

Almost the tears fell as another dart pierced her heart, but she opened her eyes the wider to hold them back and sat and sewed unwinkingly. She must not, must not cry. There was momentous thinking to be done to-night. She had not had time to consider this awful thing since it had come upon her. Was she really sure beyond a doubt that it was so? How long ago was it that she took little Celia, happy and laughing, in the trolley to the park? How little she thought what she was going out to meet as she lifted the child from the car and smilingly humored her fancy to follow a by-path through the woods. How the little feet had danced and the pretty prattle had babbled on like a tinkling brook that needed no response, but was content with its own music.

And then they had come to the edge of the park drive where they could look down upon the world of fashion as it swept along, all rubber-tired and silver-mounted, in its best array. She had sighed a happy little sigh as she surveyed a costly carriage surmounted by two servants in white and dark-green livery and saw the discontented faces of the over-dressed man and woman who sat as far apart as the width of the seat would allow, and appeared to endure their drive as two dumb animals might if this were a part of their daily round. What if she rode in state like that with a husband such as he? She had shuddered and been conscious of thankfulness over her home and her husband. What if Claude did stay away from home a good deal evenings! It was in the way of his business, he said, and she must be more patient. There would come a time by and by when he would have enough, so that they could live at their ease, and he need not go to the city ever any more. And into the midst of the bright dream she had conjured came little Celia's prattle:

"Mamma, see! Papa tummin'! Pitty lady!" She had looked down curiously to see who it was that reminded the child of her father, and her whole being froze within her. Her breath seemed not to come at all, and she had turned so ghastly white that the baby put up her hand and touched her cheek, saying, "Mamma, pitty mamma! Poor mamma!"

For there on the seat of a high, stylish cart drawn by shining black horses with arched necks, and just below a tall elegant woman, who was driving, sat her husband. Claude! Yes, little Celia's papa! Oh, that moment!

She forced herself to remember his face with its varying expressions as she had watched it till it was out of sight. There was no trouble in recalling it; it was burned into her soul with a red-hot iron. He had been talking to that beautiful woman as he used to talk to her when they were first engaged. That tender, adoring gaze; his eyes lovelighted. It was unmistakable! A heart-breaking revelation! There was no use trying to blind herself. There was not the slightest hope that he could come home and explain this away as a business transaction, or a plot between him and that other woman to draw her out into the world, or any of those pretty fallacies that might happen in books. It was all true, and she had known it instantly. It had been revealed to her as in a flash, the meaning of long months of neglect, supposed business trips, luncheons, and dinners at the club instead of the homecoming. She knew it. She ought to have seen it before. If she had not been so engrossed in her little world of the household she would have done so. Indeed, now that she knew it, she recognized also that she had been given warnings of it. Her husband had done his best to get her out. He had suggested and begged, but she had not been well during the first years of the two elder children, and the coming of the third had again filled her heart and mind. Her home was enough for her, always provided he was in it. It was not enough for him. She had tried to make it a happy one; but perhaps she had been fretful and exacting sometimes, and it may be she had been in fault to allow the children to be noisy when their father was at home.

He had always been fond of society, and had been brought up to do exactly as he pleased. It was hard for him to be shut in as she was, but that was a woman's lot. At least it was the lot of the true mother who did not trust her little ones to servants. Ah, was she excusing him? That must not be. He was her husband. She loved him deeply, tenderly, bitterly; but she would not excuse him. He was at fault, of course. He should not have been riding with a wealthy woman of fashion while his own wife came to the park on the trolley and took care of her baby as he passed by. He was not a man of wealth yet, though they had hoped he would one day be; but how did he get into this set? How came he to be sitting beside that lovely lady with the haughty air who had smiled so graciously down upon him? Her soul recoiled even now as she remembered that her husband should be looking up in that way to any woman—that is, any woman but herself—oh, no! Not even that! She wanted her husband to be a man above, far above herself. She must respect him. She could not live if she could not do that. What should she do? Was there anything to do? She would die. Perhaps that was the way out of it—she would die. It would be an easy affair. No heart could bear many such mighty grips of horror as had come upon hers that afternoon. It would not take long. But the children—her three little children! Could she leave them to the world—to another woman, perhaps, who would not love them? No, not that. Not even to save them from the shame of a father who had learned to love another woman than his wife. She reasoned this out. It seemed to her that her brain had never seen things so clearly before in all her life. Her little children were the burden of her sorrow. That all this should come upon them! A father who had disgraced them—who did not love his home! For this was certainly what it would come to be, even though he maintained all outward proprieties. She told herself that it was probable this had not been going on long. She forced herself to think back to the exact date when her husband began to stay away to dinners and to be out late evenings. How could she have been so easily satisfied in her safe, happy belief that her peace was to last forever, and go off to sleep before his return, often and often?

And then her conscience, arising from a refreshing sleep, began to take up its neglected work and accused her smartly. It was all her fault. She could see her mistakes as clearly now as if they had been roads leading off from the path she ought to have kept. She had allowed her husband to become alienated from herself. She could look back to the spot where she ought to have done something, just what she did not know. She did not even stop to question whether it had been possible in her state of health, and with their small income, which was eaten up so fast in those days by doctor's bills and little shoes. But all that was past. It could not be lived over. She had been a failure—yes, she, Miriam Hammond Winthrop—who had thought when she married that she would be the most devoted of wives, she had let her husband drift away from her, and had helped on the destruction that was coming surely and swiftly to her little children. Was it too late? Was the past utterly irretrievable? Had he gone too far? Had he lost his love for her entirely? Was her power all gone? She used to be able to bring the lovelight into his eyes. Could she ever do it again?

Suddenly she laid down the little white garment with the needle just as she was beginning to take the next stitch and went to the mirror over the mantel to look at herself.

She turned on all the gas jets and studied her face critically. Yes, she looked older, and there were wrinkles coming here and there. It seemed to her they had come that afternoon. Her eyes looked tired too, but could she not by vigorous attention to herself make her face once more attractive to her husband? If so it was worth doing, if she might save him, even if she died in the attempt. She took both hands and smoothed her forehead, rubbed her cheeks to make them red, and forgot to notice that the tears had burned themselves up, leaving her eyes brighter than usual. She tossed her hair up a little like the handsome woman's she had seen in the park. It really was more becoming. Why had she not taken the trouble to dress it in the present style? Then she went back to her chair again and took up the work. The buttonholes that she had expected would take several evenings to finish were vanishing before her excited fingers without her knowing it. It was a relief to her to do something; and she put all her energy into it so that her hands began to ache, but she was only conscious of the awful ache in her heart and sewed on.

If there were some one to advise her! Could she do it? Could she make a stand against the devil and try to save her Eden? Or was it more than one poor shy woman, with all the odds of the gay world against her, could accomplish?

She longed to have her husband come home that she might throw herself at his feet and beg and plead with him for her happiness, to save their home; she longed to accuse him madly, and fling scorching words at him, and watch his face as she told him how she and his baby had seen him that afternoon; and then she longed again to throw her arms about his neck and cry upon his breast as she used to do when they were first married, and any little thing happened that she did not like. How she used to cry over trifles then! How could she, when such a world of sorrow was coming to her so soon?

She was wise enough to know that none of these longings of her heart must be carried into effect if she would win her husband. In his present attitude he would laugh at her fears! She seemed to understand that her anguish would only anger him because he would feel condemned. Her own soul knew that she could not take him back into her heart of hearts until she won him back and he came of his own accord confessing his wrong to her. But would that ever be? He was a good man at heart, she believed. He would not do wrong, not very wrong, not knowingly. Perhaps he had not learned to love any other woman, only to love society, and—to—cease to love her.

If her dear, wise mother were there! But no! She could not tell her. She must never breathe this thing to any living soul if she would hope to do anything! His honor should be hers. She would protect him from even her own condemnation so long as she could. But what to do and how to do it!

Out of the chaos of her mind there presently began to form a plan. Her breath came and went with quick gasps and her heart beat wildly as she looked the daring thing in the face and summoned her courage to meet it.

Could she perhaps meet that woman, that outrageous woman, on her own ground and vanquish her? Could she with only the few poor little stones of her wits and the sling of her love face this woman Goliath of society and challenge her? What! expect that woman, with all her native grace and beauty, her fabulous wealth, and her years of training to give way before her? A crimson spot came out on either cheek, but she swallowed hard with her hot dry throat and set her lips in firm resolve. She could but fail. She would do it.

But how? And with what? It would take money. She could not use her husband's, at least not much of it, not to win him back. There was a little, a few hundreds, a small legacy her grandmother had left to her. How pitifully small it seemed now! She cast a glance at a fashion magazine that lay upon her table. She had bought it the day before because of a valuable article on how to make over dress skirts to suit the coming season's style. How satisfied with the sweet monotony of her life had she been then! It came to her with another sharp thrust now! But that magazine said that gowns from five to seven hundred dollars were no longer remarkable things. How she had smiled but the evening before as she read it and curled her lip at the unfortunates whose lives were run into the grooves of folly that could require such extravagance. Now she wished fiercely that she might possess several that cost not merely seven hundred but seven thousand dollars, if only she might outstrip them all and stand at the head for her husband to see.

But this was folly. She had only a little and that little must do! It had been put aside for a rainy day, or to send the children to college in case father failed. Alas! And now father had failed, but not in the way thought possible, and the money must be used to save him and them all from destruction, if indeed it would hold out. How long would it take, and how, how should she go about it?

With sudden energy she caught up the magazine and read. She had gone over it all the day before in her ride from the city where she had been shopping, and had recognized from its tone that it was familiar with a different world from hers. Now with sudden hope she read feverishly, if perchance there might be some help there for her.

Yes, there were suggestions of how to do this and that, how to plan and dress and act in the different functions of society; but of what use were they to her? How was she to begin? She was not in society and how was she to get there? She could not ask her husband. That would spoil it all. She must get there without his help.

If she only had that editor, that woman or whoever it was who answered those questions, for just a few minutes, she could find out if there was any way in which she could creep into that mystic circle where alone her battle could be fought. She had always despised people who wrote to newspapers for advice in their household troubles and now she felt a sudden sympathy for them. Actually it was now her only source of help, at least the only one of which she knew. Her cheeks burned as the suggestion of writing persistently put itself before her. She could hear her husband's scornful laugh ringing out as he ridiculed the poor fools who wrote to papers for advice, and the presumption that attempted to administer medicine—mental, moral, and physical—to all the troubles of the earth.

But the wife's heart suddenly overflowed with gratitude toward the paper. It was trying to do good in the world, it was ready to help the helpless. Why should she be ashamed to write? No one would ever know who it was. And she need not consider herself from last night's view-point. She had come to a terrible strait. Trouble and shame had entered her life. She no longer stood upon the high pinnacle of joy in happy wifehood! Her heart was broken and her idol clay. What should she care for her former ideas of nicety? It was not for her to question the ways or the means. It was for her to snatch at the first straw that presented itself, as any sensible drowning person would do.

With firm determination she laid down the magazine and walked deliberately to her desk. Her fingers did not tremble nor the resolute look pass from her chin as she selected plain paper and envelope and wrote. The words seemed to come without need of thought. She stated the case clearly in a few words, and signed her grandmother's initials. She folded, addressed the letter, and sent her sleepy little maid to post it before the set look relaxed.

Then having done all that was in her power to do that night she went up to her room in the dark and smothering her head in the pillow so that the baby should not be disturbed she let the wild sobs have their way.

CHAPTER 2

•

A Trip Abroad

"It is just barely possible I may have to take a flying trip to Paris," Claude Winthrop announced casually, looking up from the newspaper which had been engrossing his attention.

It was the next morning and his wife unrefreshed from her night's vigil was sitting quietly in her place at the breakfast table. She looked now and then at the top of her husband's head, thinking of his face as she had seen it in the park, and trying to realize that all around her was just the same outwardly as it had been yesterday and all the days that had gone before, only she knew that it was all so different.

She made some slight reply. He had said so many times that he hoped his business would take him abroad soon, that she ceased to reproach him for desiring to go without her and the children as she had done at first. She began to feel that he would not really go after all. It had been a source of uneasiness to her many times, for she had a morbid horror of having the wide ocean separate her from the one she loved better than all on earth besides. But this morning, in the light of recent discoveries, she realized that even this trouble of the past was as nothing beside what was laid upon her now to bear.

How often it is that when we mock at a trouble, or detract from its magnitude, it comes upon us suddenly as if to taunt us and reveal its true heaviness. Miriam Winthrop felt this with a sudden sharp pang a little later that day when she received and read a brief note from her husband brought by a messenger boy. For the moment all her more recent grief was forgotten and she was tormented by her former fears and dread.

"Dear Miriam," he had scrawled on the back of a business envelope, "I've got to go at once. The firm thinks I'm the only one who can represent them in Paris just now, and if I don't go there'll be trouble. I'm sorry it comes with such a rush but it's a fine thing for me. Pack my grip with what you think I need for a month. I don't want to be bothered with much. I may not get home till late and fear I shall have to take the midnight train. Haste. Claude."

She did not stop now to study the phraseology of the hastily worded note, nor let the coldness and baldness of the announcement enter her soul like a keen blade as it would be sure to do later when the trial began in dead earnest. She did not even give a thought to the difference between this note and those he used to write her when they were first married. It was enough to realize that he was going across that terrible ocean without her and talking about it as calmly as if he were but going downtown. Other people let their husbands go off without a murmur. There was Mrs. Forsythe, who smilingly said she intended to send her husband on a tour for six months so that she could be free from household cares and do as she pleased for a little while. But then she was Mr. Forsythe's wife, and Claude was—and then there came that sudden sharp remembrance of yesterday and its revelation, and her sorrow entered full into her being with a realization of what it was going to mean. Yes, perhaps she ought to be glad he was going away. But she was not—oh, she was not! It was worse a hundred-fold than it would have been if it had come two days ago. Now she was plunged into the awfulness of the black abyss that had yawned before her feet, and Claude was going from her and would not be there to help her out by any possible explanation, nor even to know of the horror in her path, for she knew in her heart that she could not and would not tell him her discovery now before he went. There would not be time, even if it were wise. No, she must bear it alone until he returned, if he ever did. Oh, that deep awful sea that must roll over her troubled heart for weeks before she could hope to begin to change things. Could she stand it? Would she live to brave it through?

A ringing baby laugh from the nursery, where Celia was drawing a wooly lamb over the floor, recalled her courage. She closed her lips in their firm lines once more and knew she would, she must!

Just one more awful thought came to her and glared at her with green, deriding, menacing eyes of possibility. That woman, could she, was she going abroad? There had been such things! Her brain reeled at the thought and with fear and wrath she put it away from her. She would never think that of Claude. No, never! She must go about making preparations for him, for there was much to be done, some mending, and where had that package of laundry been put? and, oh, the horror of having to doubt one's husband! Claude might have been injudicious, but never wicked! No! She was unworthy to be his wife when she could think such things with absolutely nothing to found them upon save a simple everyday ride in the park. She hurried upstairs to bureau drawers and sent the nurse and the maid-of-all-work flying about on various errands and herself worked with swift, skilled fingers. But all the time the ache grew in her heart till it seemed it must break.

He did not come home to lunch. She had not expected that. She scarcely stopped herself to making a pretence of eating. So eager was she to complete the little things she had thought of to do for his comfort during the voyage before he should return that she forgot herself entirely in her present duties. The stinging tears welled up to her eyes without falling as they had done the night before, and burned themselves dry, again and again, and still she worked on feverishly, adding other little touches to the preparations she had made. He should not have cause for impatience that she had forgotten anything in his thought of her during the trip. She even put in his old cap that he was fond of wearing in traveling and which heretofore she had always struggled to secrete safely before they set out for a journey. There

was a fine disregard of self in all that she did about the
suit-case and a close attention to details of his liking. If
he had any thought left for her at all he could not fail to
note it.

She carefully placed a leather photograph case, a present from the children on last Christmas, containing all
their likenesses with hers, in an inner pocket with his
handkerchiefs, and then on second thought took it out
to remove her own face and put in its place a new pose
of the baby. She would not seek to remind him thus of
her. He should see that she no longer put in any claims
for his affection. Just why she did this she could not
explain to herself, but she felt a triumph over herself in
having done it. Was it revenge or love or jealousy or all?
She did not know. She sat down beside the completed
work and let great drops fall on the heavy, unresponsive
leather, and groaned aloud, and then got up hastily to
wipe her eyes and flash them in defiance at herself in the
mirror. She would not give way now. She must act her
part till he was gone. Then she would weep until she
could get relief enough to think and know what to do.

He came late to dinner and brought his secretary with
him. During the meal they were going over certain business matters which were to be left in this young man's
charge. Miriam presided over her table and supplied
their needs and held her tongue, feeling in this brief
time of quietness and inaction how weary she was, how
every nerve quivered with pain, how her eyeballs stung,
and how the little veins in her temples throbbed.

They went to the library after dinner, where there was
more business. The wife went up to her nursery and
hovered over her daily cares, which suddenly seemed to
have lost their necessity, so much greater was her need
of some word with her husband.

It was not till ten o'clock that the front door closed
upon the young man of business and she heard Claude
coming upstairs. Her heart leaped then. Would he possibly say something comforting to her, some word of
love for her, now that he was leaving, some little regret
that she could not go too? Something, perhaps, that
might explain that awful sight of yesterday, and wipe

this day out of existence for her so far as its suffering had been concerned? Oh, if that might be she would never murmur again at sorrow or loneliness or anything that could come upon her, so long as she could have her husband her own.

But no, that could not be, she knew, for there was that look that she had seen her husband give to the strange woman, and even as she thought she heard him go into the bedroom.

"Miriam," he called, without waiting for her to come to the door, "I'm going right to bed. I'm just about played out, and I'll have to start early in the morning. Have you got everything all fixed up? All right, then I'll turn in. Don't let any one disturb me. I've told Simmons about everything, and if any call comes from the office folks you can refer them to Simmons."

Her low murmured "All right," was followed by the quick closing door. She stood in the hall and heard him move about the room, and knew that she might go to him and tell him all, or get some word from him more than this before he slept to wake and rush away from her, but she would not. She heard the click of the light as he turned it out, and the silence that followed his lying down, and reflected that she might at least go and kiss him good-night, and yet she had not the power to move.

How long she stood there she did not know. It seemed to her that every action of her life since she had known her husband came and was enacted before her, that every word he had ever spoken or written to her was spoken distinctly in her ear. She felt again his power over her when he told her how he loved her, and the gladness that enwrapped her like a garment as she knew that she loved him. It turned to a pall now as the other thoughts of yesterday trooped up, death-faced and horrid, to mock at those happier times.

She roused herself by and by to see that the house was locked for the night and the children sleeping quietly as usual. Then she made a careful toilet for the morning. It would need to be freshened a little she knew, if she could manage it, but the main points must be looked after now when her mind was clear. She must leave upon her husband a fair memory, a pleasing vision, if indeed this poor heartsick body of hers could be made to look pleasant to any one.

She put on a more elaborate gown than she had been wont to consider proper for a morning dress, but it was her husband's favorite color. She disregarded all her former prejudices and scorned her economies. What were economies when life was at stake? She also arranged her hair in the new way, taking a long time at it and being very critical of herself. All the while this was going on she was conscious of trying to stop thinking and to absorb herself in her occupation. The color was high in her cheeks. Her night of vigil and her day of labor, followed by the disappointment that her husband had said no tender word to her, had brought a feverishness which heightened the brilliancy of her eyes. She could see that she looked young again, and drew a little hope from the fact.

But a toilet cannot last a night-time even with such precious ends at stake, and when it was finished she took a candle and stole silently into the bedroom.

She had known that this moment must come. Her heart would not let her let him go without it. She must look down upon him and remember all the past and know the present with his face in sight. She had been dreading it and putting it off ever since he had shut the door. Now she stood and looked at him as he lay sleeping.

He was handsome even in his sleep. His heavy dark hair was tossed back against the pillow and his broad forehead looked noble to her even now with all the tumult surging in her heart against him. She noted the long black lashes, the same his little children had. He looked so young as he lay asleep, and she could see their oldest child's resemblance to him as she had never seen it before. She made herself take in every feature. The pleasant curves of the lips, those lips that had said kind words, tender words of love to her, and had kissed her—and alas, could frame themselves in impatience. She could see them now as they looked during a recent disagreement. The remembrance struck like a blow across her heart. His arms were thrown out over the bed in the abandonment of weariness, and his hands seemed to appeal to her for a kindly thought. Those white hands, so symmetrical, and yet so firm and strong, how she had admired them as a girl. How proud she had always been of them as his wife. How they had helped her own hands when they first began their life together. She fain would stoop and kiss just his hand. She could not let him go without. He was tired, so tired; and she was sorry, so sorry; and he was her husband! She set the candle down softly upon the floor at a little distance and stooped, but started up at a suggestion. Had that hand ever touched in gentle pressure the hands of other women? Did that other woman know those shapely hands, that were hers, and yet were not hers now? She bowed her head amid the draperies of the bed and almost groaned aloud. She would fain have prayed, as there was no other help at hand, but she was not a praying woman. True she had a habit of kneeling to repeat a form of words, but even that form failed her now, though she tried to find some words to voice a cry to the Unknown.

Was ever sorrow like unto hers? Were there in the world other women who suffered this sort of thing? Yes, of course there were, there must be, poor wretches; she had read of them and known of them always; poor creatures who could not keep, or never had, their husbands' love; but not such as she, and such as Claude; no, no, that could not be! This never had happened before. It could not be true! She would not believe it. There must be some mistake.

The long night passed at last, and the toilet given its final touches, though the face it was meant to set off was wan with sorrow and exhaustion. Very quietly she served the breakfast, which was a hasty meal, as there was little time. She nerved herself to be bright and unconcerned, as if the proposed journey were but a brief one for a few hours. She had been wont to grieve so deeply at thought of separation, that her husband wondered a little that she should take it so quietly, and if he had had more time to note her and less upon his mind he would have seen the abnormal state of excitement that kept her calm and smiling when her heart was so fiercely torn.

Miriam saw to it that the children were at hand at the last moment to be kissed good-bye, and then with a hasty word of some handkerchiefs she had forgotten to put in his grip she flew up the stairs and locked her door. She could not bear the hasty farewell, the careless kiss she saw was coming. She preferred that he should leave her uncaressed.

"Come, Miriam, I must go. Don't wait for handkerchiefs. There's no time to look. The cab is at the door. Come."

But she did not come, and he called good-bye and went.

She watched him slam the cab door after him and drive away in the early morning light, and then the great sobs that had been so carefully choked down for hours came and shook her frame, and she hid her face in the pillows where he had slept but a little while ago and let her sorrow wave upon wave roll over her head and bury her in the awful chasms between its breakers till kindly nature claimed the worn-out body and over-wrought nerves, and wrapt her in a deep and dreamless sleep of utter weariness.

CHAPTER 3

•

An Important Letter

•

The days that followed were to her like a long struggle
through the darkness of some deep valley by night.
When she looked back upon them they were filled with
horror. Every time she slept and awoke there was the
same awful realization of trouble to be instantly remembered and realized, coming with the keenness of first
knowledge during the earliest waking moments, as one
remembers death or dread calamity and tries to weave
the unaccustomed threads of sorrow into the hitherto
happy web of life and make it seem a part of the daily
fabric.

She plunged into work with all her soul and body.
What was to come she had yet to discover. She felt that
now her course lay clear before her, she had but to get
out of the way any work that might be a hindrance to the
plans when they should be formed. The children's
clothes were first. She had been working at them lei-
surely for some time, taking pleasure in designing and
executing the pretty, dainty garments which should
make her children into picturesque little creatures. Now
she set about finishing this work with feverish eagerness and conscientiousness. She foresaw that her tender
care of these little ones must be interrupted in future.
What had been her duty and her pleasure must now be
neglected for a higher, more insistent duty, which could
not be delayed.

She put lingering, wistful touches on her work and a
world of love and pent-up mother desires. This much

she could do before the demand for action came and she would do it better than it had ever been done before. But there was also another reason for the care she put upon the little garments. When she remembered this her face was almost bitter in its stern determination and her fingers flew the faster. She was going out to fight the world, and the world, if she succeeded, would be free to inspect her life, her home, her children, everything she had. These same little chores of theirs would not escape the inspection. They were to be a part of her furnishing for the warfare in which she was to engage. Therefore she worked late and early, and in a surprisingly short time the garments were laid away complete for use.

One of the first things she had done during these days of work had been to write a letter subscribing for the "Fashion Magazine," to which she had sent her appeal for help. She felt that she simply could not go to a newsstand and buy it. Her shame, her disgrace would be written large upon her face. No, she must make sure to see it if any answer appeared to her letter, but she must see it first in the quiet and seclusion of her own room with locked doors. Whenever, as she went back and forth to the city stores, she saw a copy of that magazine in a window or a notice of it upon a sign-board, she turned her face guiltily away. It was as if the name of it was shouted to her from afar. She dreaded the thought that any one should know to what depths she had descended, actually to have written to a public editor for assistance in her trouble. And yet, and yet in spite of it all and without her own consent, she was building greatly on the answer that should come to her. Would they understand what she wanted? And would they give her any help that she could follow? Or would she have to go blindly all alone? This thought gradually began to stand out clearly in her confused brain as she tried to plan while her fingers were executing wonders with her needle.

A month! And she must be ready for action when her husband returned. It might be he would be delayed longer, but she must be ready. Would the printed help come in time? How long did it take those things to get to headquarters and fall into line with other questions till at last an answer could come?

She watched the mail from week to week. The day of the arrival of the magazine was an anxious one. She shivered when it was put into her hand and tried to go about her household duties calmly, forcing herself to give the cook minute directions sometimes before retiring behind locked doors to scan the pages hastily and then more thoroughly. It must not be suspected that she had more than a passing interest in that magazine.

She read every word from cover to cover to make sure she did not miss her answer, though she knew such answers only appeared in a certain column. Meantime she was gaining much worldly knowledge as she read. There was a certain "shibboleth" spoken in those columns which she foresaw she must make her own if she would be the success she aimed to be. Unconsciously she weighed this and that question in dress, household decoration, manners, and customs. Without her own knowledge she grew to apply these newly acquired rules to her own home and life.

At last one morning she found the initials she had signed to her question staring her in the face.

For one brief instant she closed her eyes and drew a deep breath. Then her hand fluttered to her heart and she read with nervous rapidity:

Indeed, I have considered the situation carefully, for I know exactly what a complex problem you feel you have to face. But let me reassure you; many and many a wife and mother is in a similar predicament. How can it be otherwise when one has since marriage had little children to take care of and is occupied in the most natural, best of all ways that a woman can be occupied?

Miriam Winthrop caught her breath in a quick, dry sob at this, and then read on:

But I must congratulate you for the conclusion you have reached and your wise, wholesome desire to take up social life again and make a position for yourself and your husband, and, above all, for your children's future.

Ah, yes, for her children's future! But not in the way the writer meant.

It seems to me it would be unwise to start out to entertain elaborately even if you have the means for it. No, I should not advise you to give a big general reception, nor big dinners, nor anything of the sort. First of all, it would be inappropriate to entertain so in your small house, for you know there is proportion in everything. But what you could do is to send out cards for four days next month, let us say.

Then followed minute directions for the giving of informal little teas, with details of simple refreshments, decorations, forms, and costumes suggested. Nothing was forgotten, though there were no superfluous words used, from the garb and deportment of the maid who opens the door to directions about the proper garments for her husband to wear. Ah, her husband knew to an exact science how to dress well upon all possible occasions. That one suggestion was unnecessary, and a deep sigh was breathed in her excitement as she read on, more and more convinced that the beginning of the undertaking seemed possible.

There was also a plan of further campaign of dinners and luncheons and a children's party hinted at, and the writer concluded:

Meanwhile you will probably receive invitations in return which you should accept, wearing pretty, becoming dresses to the entertainments and making as much of yourself as possible. This is every woman's duty, especially if she is a wife and mother. Try to read up on the subjects which are generally talked of, so that you will be an intelligent companion besides educating yourself, and try to find out what are the interests of the people you want to know. Return your calls regularly. When you have established a position for yourself it will be perfectly permissible for you, when you meet a stranger at a luncheon, or dinner, or any entertainment at the house of a mutual friend, to ask her if you may not call, as you would like to know her better, so gradually you will enlarge your circle without forcing yourself. I should advise you, if you have time, to go into some charitable work; join one of the societies of your church, and do what you can to help others outside of your home. By and by send out cards for a series of days and give during the winter some *musicales* or readings, if you can afford them. I am very certain you will succeed in your undertakings. It only requires tact and thought for others.

She closed her eyes and leaned back in her chair with another deep sigh as suddenly the appalling magnitude of the work she had undertaken broke over her. She faltered at the thought of the wearisome way she must tread. Would it all pay? Could she do it? Would her strength and her money hold out till she gained her point and won her husband to herself? Was it not worse than useless to try? Might she not better give in at the start and accept the situation? Never!

She sprang to her feet, throwing the magazine down and walking excitedly to and fro, her hot brain fairly reeling under the whirl of plans for sandwiches and dresses and invitations and sundries which should cost but a trifle and yet should hold their own with the best.

And from that moment she went forward and would not *think* the word defeat. She had a clue to the ways of the great world. It had been given her graciously and clearly. She could understand and obey. She felt in her heart that there would be results. If there was failure, it would be her fault in carrying out instructions; but there *should not* be failure. She would see to that. Had she not always been able to make or do anything that she had set her heart upon? She recalled with a weary smile how she had patiently sewed white feathers on an old ivory fan frame as a girl, because her dearest wish had been to have a feather fan and her mother had not considered their purse was full enough for such an unnecessary expenditure. There were other things too, small in them-

selves, but as she looked back upon them and recalled
how she had carried her point despite all obstacles, they
gave her courage to hope that what she had once done
she could do again. Her purpose should be carried out
to the end. It was her only hope. Then with a pitiful sob
trembling in her throat as she drew another deep breath
she unlocked her door and walked forth to begin her
herculean task.

Downtown her resolves led her, to the great stores,
where were wonders of the world of fashion in plenty.
Her money was limited and she must use her wits.

It happened to be a good day for her induction into
the science that began in the garden of Eden with a fig
leaf. That was a brilliant exhibition of gowns, robes,
dresses, frocks, or whatever the fashionable name for
the outer covering a woman wears happened to be that
week, and the display of more bewildering beauty of texture, color, form and fashion than perhaps had ever
been seen in that city before.

She paused before the great glass cases containing
these marvels of the dressmakers' art and began a systematic study, catching her breath at the enormous im-
portance that the world placed upon clothes, and then
shutting her eyes to her own stupendous audacity.

She went over all the beautiful display once and then
returned to the beginning and began to take notes in
minute detail. There was that great exquisite gray costume. There were possibilities in her own gray silk, out
of date and somewhat worn. She noted carefully the little touch of elegance given by the vest of latticed gray
velvet ribbon, the spaces filled by filmy spider's webs in
silver thread. Being well versed in lace stitches she took
courage. That vest which alone gave the costume its dis-
tinguishment would be unattainable to most women
without a well-filled purse. To her it was quite possible.
Her skillful fingers would help her here with little labor.
The real outer material of the garment need not be expensive, some light wool with silken threads, and lined
with her old gray silk. She drew a sigh of relief and
passed on, mentally counting the few dollars that would
represent this first dress. There would not be many such

for she had but few silk dresses that would even do for lining. There was a black one which might work in, and that was all, unless she sacrificed her wedding gown. She almost blushed to think of its simplicity beside the billows of white satin she at that moment came upon, encrusted with priceless point lace. She passed it by with a mere glance and moved on to another simple-looking costume which scarcely seemed to belong to the elaborate collection, and appeared almost to be shrinking behind the card announcing its designer and executor. Mrs. Winthrop read the card. Not for nothing had she studied her fashion magazine. She knew the name of that house in Paris well by this time, and stood in awe before the model of cloth that was representative. She looked from the card back to the gown and began to see detail such as she had read about and until now had not understood. What gladdened her more than anything else was to discover that most of the distinguishing features of these wonderful dresses were bits of needle work which could easily be attained by one who understood embroidery and lace making and all the many little arts and secrets of fancy work of the higher grade as did she. She blessed the days gone by when she had let her happy fingers learn this cunning while she framed wonderful stories of bears and fairies and poppy-garlanded nymphs from the land of sweet dreams for her little ones. Oh, in those days, she had never conceived of the terrible need in which these accomplishments would bring her aid!

But she must not pause to let these thoughts sweep over her and bring that terrible grip of her heart which seemed almost like a piercing dagger. She must control her feelings. She would have need of a heart strong and active for her work. She must not let it break down for lack of self-control. She had heard that great trouble would bring on heart disease. She would not let it come to her. Her will should lay an iron hand upon her feelings and keep her laughing and bright in spite of the shadow that lurked just over her head. She would force her body to perform all the physical part of being glad. It might be there was something in the mind cure. She had

read of such things. She would try it. Not try, she would
make it succeed. Steadily on she went around that array
again, growing interested as she progressed, putting
down in a little note-book, items to be remembered, re-
lating to certain things she might do with old material or
with her ability to embroider and sew.

She ignored many showy wax ladies in imported at-
tire as being out of keeping with her needs. There was
one sentence in her mentor's letter she had not forgotten: "for you know there is proportion in everything." It
should never be said of her that she was inappropriately
dressed for her position. Everything should be quiet
and yet—and yet—cunning planner—she meant to
have the distinguished, inimitable something about her
clothes that would mark the woman of good taste in the
art of dressing well, and give a dim idea of studied plain-
ness which every well-dressed woman knows is purchased at far greater price than the more showy
garment. Once she paused beside a lovely creation of
point lace whose pattern was faintly outlined in the tin-
iest possible ruched ribbon of pale pink, like a dream of
roses in winter frost, and examined the pattern, while
the wax-cheeked bridesmaid who wore it graciously
held out a wilderness of pink roses before her unnoticing eyes, and surveyed her staringly from under her
thick auburn eyelashes. She studied the lace carefully
and wondered if she could achieve its like for the gar-
nishing of one of her gowns with a collar and handkerchief of fine point she possessed, and some of that
delicate ribbon work. How effective it would be on black!

Weary at last of the long strain she turned to go back.
She would just see that gray suit again to be sure how
the white chiffon was arranged under the gray and silver lattice and the exact shade of the canary colored
breast knot of soft satin, and then she would go home
for that day. She was too tired to do another thing, and
really she had accomplished much. She must have a
sample of her own gray silk before she could get the
outer material. What a blessing that the gray silk waist
fitted her beautifully. All the better that it was plain. It
would make a most delightful lining. Of course the skirt

must be remodeled but that would not be difficult with a good pattern. She could do the underpart all herself and not have a dressmaker till she was ready for the outside. Ah! perhaps she might even accomplish this one gown alone entirely. She was sure she could do all the particular parts if she gave herself up to it, and that would leave more money to pay for the other things, for the dressmaker would have much to do and she must go to a very good one to have her linings made, and perhaps to a tailor for some things. She must economize all she could.

Thinking which she arrived before the gray gown.

Then from above her, somewhere on another floor of the great store and floating down through the open rotunda, came soft, sweet, swelling music, like angelic voices from afar.

It seemed to come nearer and surround her being and float about her naked soul and bathe her in its restfulness.

In a distant gallery there was some newly invented instrument, by whose mechanism a thousand harps and voices seemed to be set free at once and soar aloft in blended harmony.

The melody was familiar. It had been dear to her when it first came out. She knew the words. Each note spoke to her heart now. It had grown tiresomely familiar during her stay in this part of the world, by the constant grinding of it out by the poor wheezy street pianos and hand-organs, as if a common barnyard fowl should attempt the thrush's roundelay. But now the song seemed to come to her with new significance.

> Last night I lay a sleeping,
>   There came a dream so fair,
> I saw the Holy City
>   Beside the temple there,
> I heard the children singing
>   And ever as they sang
> Methought the voice of angels
>   From heaven in answer rang,
>   Jerusalem, Jerusalem.

The burdened woman looking up, startled suddenly from her intricate busy plans for earth, realized almost with a sort of mingled horror and longing that there was another world than this. Would what she did now and here affect her happiness there? Would these poor paltry dresses count? Would her trouble be over ever?

Her throat choked up and she stood leaning against the glass case unheeding the people who passed and looked curiously at her absorbed, listening face.

When the music was over she went home.

CHAPTER 4

•

Her Rival Disclosed

That night she dreamed a single dream the whole night through. The scene reminded her of the background of some posters. There was a sky of clearly defined blotches of inky blue and dead white, with strange angels outlined against it. They seemed to be constantly warning her against something, at command of heavenly music that floated above, now soft, now clearer, as the need became greater. And she below, was striving to obey, with anguish in her soul. Gradually the face of her husband appeared a little way off, smiling, glad, gay. He was talking with a throng of beautiful women and evil men. Then it became clear that the danger was to him, and the angels were bidding her save him.

With all her soul dragging her down in heaviness she sought to get nearer to him and to attract his attention, but his expressive eyes rested on all faces but hers. He did not see, or would not recognize her. Her soul longed for one loving smile such as he used to give her in the old days when they were in a company of friends and could not speak save with their eyes. But now he would not look. He seemed to be another being and yet the same. At last she could lay her hand upon his and then she thought he surely would look, and she poured out pleading words into his ear of warning and entreaty. But he shook her off with anger, passed on from her grasp, and with a cry which seemed to rend her heart she awoke to live the whole scene over again.

Out from a night thus spent she went to her task, with

white face and set lips. That gray dress should be
bought to-day and begun.

She wasted no time in looking that morning. But as
she sat waiting at the counter for a package which she
wished to take home with her, a woman, tall and ele-
gantly gowned, moved slowly down the aisle and
stopped close beside her to examine an exquisite piece
of lace that was being displayed.

Some sudden memory made Mrs. Winthrop look up
at her face, and there she saw before her the one who
had sat beside her husband in the park but a few days
before.

Her heart fairly stood still to think that that woman
was beside her. A great wave of hate and horror rolled
over her and threatened for a moment to take away her
consciousness, but her self-control that morning was tremendous, and she compelled her eyes to look steadily at
the one who had won her husband from her, perhaps,
but who, after all, was but a woman, another like herself. She would see what it was that had attracted. Oh, if
she could but find out who she was!

And as if in answer to her wish came a smiling saleswoman, saying: "Good morning, Mrs. Sylvester. Is any
one waiting upon you?"

Miriam, quietly waiting for her package, sat watching
her supposed rival as she tumbled the laces about
ruthlessly as though their yards were priced in pennies
instead of dollars, and at last ordered home two pieces
that she might the better decide which suited her. As
she moved away the smiling saleswoman said, "Let me
see; the number is 1820 is it not? I cannot remember anything this morning," and the proud lady bent her head
and smiled condescendingly in reply and then swept by
and was gone.

Mrs. Winthrop turned feverish eyes to the busy pencil
that was rapidly writing down the address and noted
carefully the name of the fashionable square where Mrs.
Sylvester lived. Then she gathered up her packages and
started home, her knees trembling under her as she
walked and a quiver ran through her as if she had faced
her worst foe.

Suddenly she stopped in the street and a light broke over her face. There was a rift, just a little rift in the dark clouds over her head. And now she knew that down deep in her heart she had harbored a fear which she would not let be put into thoughts even, that this woman, this enemy of hers, this Mrs. Sylvester, was on the wide ocean. Nay, even that she might be in the same ship with her own husband, Claude. Now that she knew she was not she saw the absurdity of the idea. That a woman who calmly purchased such costly lace would give up her great orbit for the sake of a comparatively poor man was ridiculous. Still, there were women who liked to play with hearts, and who took care never to play the game too long with any one. And after all, what mattered it whether she played it well or ill, so long as the other player had been willing. Ah! That was the hard part. Her Claude was hers no longer. He had given another woman the light of his eyes, and his wife's heart was breaking. The tiny gleam of light in the clouds above closed blank and dull once more and she went on her way with a tumult of feelings running riot in her breast.

An idea came to her as she took her way home which startled her with its daring. What if she should try to use this very woman to help against herself? How could she do it? What sort of woman was she? What if she should invite her to one of these little teas for which she was preparing? What if she should? What if she *should?* Then would she not be going forth to meet Goliath the Great with her little sling and stones?

But the thought could not be got rid of. Thereafter every gown she planned, every fabric she bought or fashioned, every arrangement of the little home was done as under the surveillance of the haughty, beautiful woman with the scornful mouth and unscrupulous eyes.

The days that followed were weary ones, scarce begun ere ended, it seemed to the poor woman who was toiling to achieve a multiplicity of works before a certain time. She worked with breathless energy, never daring to stop and rest lest she should give up and faint be-

neath the load, or lest the tragedy of her life should
wreck her mind.

Letters came from her husband as he went from place
to place. A few directions were given her about matters
of business, but they always seemed to be written in
haste. Her fingers trembled when she opened them and
her heart grew colder at each one she read. He complained of not receiving her letters and she set her lips
grimly, which ill became the softly rounded lines of
mouth and chin. She had written none, nor would she.
The questions he asked might be answered when he
came. They seemed to be of moment to him, to her they
were as trifles. The questions he did *not* ask were a
whole volume of the tragedy she was living. The fact that he
did not think or care to ask them made her excuse for not
writing; though her heart was sometimes bursting with
the words she would send him, still she restrained herself. It was not time yet. She must bide and work and be
ready when the moment came.

A goodly array of "soft apparel" was gathering in her
wardrobe. Under constant supervision the housemaid
was growing silent and dextrous in the matter of waiting
upon doors and tables. She wondered in her heart why
her mistress had suddenly grown so punctilious about
the wearing of caps and aprons and a silver tray for the
cards.

There were various changes made in the house. The
amount of money spent was not large but the changes
were an improvement. A carpenter and an upholsterer
for a few hours, with some yards of effective material, a
good supply of paint and an artistic eye had really meta-
morphosed the home into a charming spot. Mrs.
Winthrop visited noted decorators, and wandered with
attentive eye through the model rooms in housefurnish-
ing establishments until she was well versed in the
effects aimed at by the highest artists in that line. She
had faithfully followed the advice of her magazine to
study her rooms from different points of view and make
them express something beautiful from every one, and
the effect was really lovely, although to her it spoke of
but one thing—her great sorrow. There was nothing

gaudy or imposing about the pleasant little house. All was in keeping with its surroundings, but there was not a spot that did not suggest restfulness, brightness, a cheery place in which to chat, an inviting nook to read a book. She certainly had succeeded beyond her highest hopes in making her home an attractive one to the guests she proposed to bring there, but the wonder was that she had succeeded when the real feelings in her heart had been anything but restfulness and peace and joy, the elements of a true home.

And then came the question of the guests. Ah, those guests. Who were they to be? It had seemed easy to get into society by the purchase of a few gowns and the arrangement of her house, with the sending out of the mysterious bits of white pasteboard which meant so much in society. But first, who was society, the society into which she must get to win her point? And how was she to find out? Her husband could tell her. Of course he knew all about it, but it would not do to ask him. If she had done as he wished when they were first married and gone hither and yon and entertained, all might have been different. Perhaps she would have held her own with him if she had done so. Doubtless their money would have been inadequate for such a life, but then too, doubtless many things would have been different. It was too late to think of what might have been. It was too late to go to her husband for help to undo her past. She must accomplish her task alone.

Then she sat down with determined mien to surmount this new difficulty in her path. She thought over the list of her acquaintances. There was just one person, and she could scarce be called an acquaintance, upon whose presence she was determined, if it was possible to compass it, and that person was Mrs. Sylvester. What sort of a woman she was, how she would accept society—such society as Mrs. Claude Winthrop could offer her—and how society—the kind of society that was Mrs. Winthrop's ideal—would accept Mrs. Sylvester, were questions that forced themselves upon her thoughts continually and which she compelled herself to put away. She could not answer them. It was better for her that they were not answered, for have Mrs. Sylvester she would, and after all, when danger and chance of mistake were on every hand in this unknown way, what mattered a few little questions like that? She had nothing to lose and everything to gain. Therefore Mrs. Sylvester's name and address, carefully remembered, headed the list when she set herself to make it out.

Then there were her neighbors. She thought them carefully over. Not one of them was what she would call a society woman, for theirs was not a fashionable street. There was the woman across the way who slapped her baby and the woman on her right who wore such a horrible bonnet and the one on her left who borrowed butter and sugar and eggs over the back fence and talked bad English and called her husband always "He." The would-be hostess shivered and let her mind travel rapidly up the street and down again on the other side, and decided that there was only one eligible neighbor on it and she a quiet, sweet-faced, elderly woman, who dressed plainly and lived alone with a niece, a pretty girl whose tasteful fingers allowed her always to be dressed well. With a defiant thought toward Mrs. Sylvester and a remembrance that her husband had once said they were the only really intellectual people on the street, she wrote down the name of the Winslows.

Then she bit her pencil and thought again. There were the ladies of the church who had called upon her when she first moved to that place several years ago, and who had continued to call at long intervals apparently from a sense of duty. They were not society people, but were wealthy and dressed well and would do her no discredit. She certainly owed them a social debt if she owed it to any one in the whole city. One after another she wrote their names hesitatingly, her face troubled meanwhile. These were not the kind of people who could help her much in what she had to do. There were others in the church where they had gone, regularly at first and then more seldom, till now they scarcely went at all. It was a large church and fashionable. Yes, and there were society people in it. Religion was fashionable sometimes. She had met a few, but would she dare invite such people on so slight acquaintance? Mrs. Sylvester was different. She was to be invited anyway. But these others. There were the Lymans and the Whartons and the Bidwells and a dozen other families. Stay, did not her magazine help her there? It suggested that she attend some of the charities of her church. Perhaps there she would become better acquainted. But what were they and how was she to find out? She must go to church and discover.

She leaned wearily back in her chair and drew her hands nervously across her eyes. It was Saturday evening, and she had been feeling thankful that it was a disgrace to sew on the Sabbath and she could have a little time to rest, but here came another duty looming up for that day also. There was no help for it, however. She saw that she must go and begin to get acquainted.

Back flew her pencil to her paper and down went the names of the best families in her church, with an inward resolve to come home from the service the next day with an introduction to some of them, if it were a possible thing, and a list of all the meetings of the church at which she would be likely to meet them. Poor little woman. She did not know how few, how pitifully few, of these best families attended the different meetings of the church. Well for her that she did not, for she counted much on those "charities" that she was to take up for bringing her friends, and one more straw that night might have broken her down, she was so near to discouragement.

There came a memory now of men her husband called great, men he had met and some he wished to meet. She wrote their names all down, wondering gravely if there was any way in which she could get to know them well enough to invite them to her home. One in particular, a man well known in political circles and whose speeches in the United States House of Representatives had become famous. She suddenly remembered a much-neglected cousin of her mother's living in another part of the city who had an intimate acquaintance with this great man, being an old schoolmate of his sister. Perhaps she could help. At any rate she must be invited. Her cheek crimsoned at the thought that she had been forgotten, and she drew her breath quickly as she wondered what Aunt Katharine would think of Mrs. Sylvester.

Then there were a few literary people well known to Aunt Katharine. Down went their names and up came Aunt Katharine in her niece's estimation as her heart began to lighten. Counting up, she saw she had a goodly list if—that great if—if they all came.

The little cuckoo clock that had been a cherished wedding gift came out and sang twelve times in the hallway, and Mrs. Winthrop, remembering with a sigh the hour of church and that morning was already upon her, put the list in her desk and went to bed, wondering as she closed her aching eyes if the days would ever be over when all this horror would be a thing of the past and she could lie down in quietness and peace and truly rest.

CHAPTER 5

·

An Unexpected Service

Mrs. Winthrop had hurried to church late and seated herself a little flurried over a new gown she wore, which seemed to her not to fit just right. She was anxious to put on her bravest front before the world in this her first approach for its favor. She bowed her head in reverent attitude, but her mind was still intent upon the problem which had occupied it on the way to church—whether she could achieve the making of a certain gown described in her last fashion magazine without any more help than the picture and her own wits. She raised her head and sat back in her seat as the text was announced:

"See, saith he, that thou make all things according to the pattern shewed to thee in the mount."

The words startled her. They could not have sounded to her soul more loudly if they had been, "See that thou make all things according to the patterns showed to thee in the fashion magazine."

Indeed, when the sentence first reached her ear, her overstrained imagination fancied the preacher was speaking to her, had read her thought, and was about to administer a reproof. Her color rose and she glanced nervously about.

But there was on every face about her a well bred apathy that betokened perfect trust in the ability of the speaker to perform his part of the services without disturbing them.

Mrs. Winthrop tried now to center her mind on what was being said. Perhaps she had mistaken his words and her own silly brain had falsified the text to suit what was in her mind.

When a third time came the words: "See . . . that thou make all things according to the pattern shewed to thee in the mount!" it began to seem an awful sentence, though without any very distinct meaning.

The sermon which followed was eloquent and learned. There was an elaborate description of the tabernacle, and the main point of the sermon, if point there might be said to be, was an appeal for certain styles of church architecture. But of all this Mrs. Claude Winthrop heard not a word, except it might have been the name of Moses.

In her younger days she had been taught the Bible. She knew in a general way that "the mount" was something holy. She did not wait to puzzle her brain about Moses in the mount nor wonder what it was he had been given a pattern of. She might have recalled it if she had tried. But instead she simply took the text as spoken to her. There had been something unearthly, almost uncanny, to her weary brain in the way the words had been said out of the stillness that came after the singing had ceased. In her uneasy state of mind it was brought home to her how far from any patterns given in any mounts had been the things that she had made of late.

Following close upon the benediction came the bewilderment of a familiar greeting. Mrs. Winthrop had been so beset by her thoughts during the sermon that she had thus far lost sight of her object in coming to church that morning. True, she grasped in her hand, as if it were something precious, the church calendar containing the announcements of all meetings of the church to be held that week, but she had forgotten to look out among the congregation those who might help in her schemes. Therefore she stood in amazement at the torrent of words spoken by the young girl who had sat in the seat before her. She knew that the girl's name was Celia Lyman and that her mother belonged to an exclusive set of people. She had barely a speaking acquaintance with Mrs. Lyman, and had never felt that she would be likely to recognize her outside of the church.

"I beg your pardon," the sweet voice said, while a detaining gloved hand was laid gently on Miriam's arm, "but mamma told me to be sure and give you a message. She was unable to get out this morning. She has one of her miserable headaches, and is all worn out. But she wanted me to tell you that she was anxious to have you come to our house Thursday to the *musicale*. She supposed she had sent you an invitation with the rest, but this morning she found it had slipped down behind her writing desk against the wall. She remembers laying it out for Miss Faulkes to look up your street and number, for mamma had quite forgotten it—she never remembers such things—but there it lay with only your name on it. And now Miss Faulkes says she couldn't find your address and forgot to speak to mamma about it. She is becoming careless about things. So as it was so late and mamma could not find the paper with your address she thought maybe you would just take the invitation informally this time, for there is to be some really fine music which mamma is sure you will enjoy. You won't mind this once, will you?" and a pair of violet eyes searched her face as if the matter were of great moment.

Mrs. Winthrop endeavored to veil her amazement and murmured her thanks, saying that the manner of the invitation did not matter, and was rewarded by a most ravishing smile.

"Then you'll be sure to come. Four to six is the hour. Oh, and I had almost forgotten, mamma told me to be sure to get your street and number so it would be on hand for another time of need," and a dainty silver pencil and silver mounted memoranda was lifted from a collection of small nothings that hung on tiny chains at her belt, while the lovely eyes were lifted to her face inquiringly.

Mrs. Winthrop was conscious of a slight lifting of Miss Celia's eyebrows as she repeated the street and number after her and wrote, and was there just a shadow of surprise in her voice? It was not a fashionable locality, and Miriam Winthrop suddenly saw a new difficulty in her way.

Then she turned to go down the aisle and bowed here

and there mechanically, scarcely knowing whom she met. How strange, how very strange, that Mrs. Lyman, after almost two years of utterly ignoring her since they had first met, should suddenly invite her to her home and her wonderful *musicales*, for their fame had reached even her ears, stranger almost though she was. It must be that a Higher Power was enlisted to help her to-day, for here was opening to her the very door the key of which she had despaired of finding. A superstitious feeling that the text was meant for her in some way as a warning, kept clinging to her, and made her go to her own room as soon as she had reached home, and after bolting her door kneel down and whisper a few words that were meant for a sort of prayer, an attempt to placate some unseen Ruler in whom she believed with a sort of nursery-fairy-tale credulity.

In the meantime Miss Celia Lyman was detailing her encounter to her mother.

"Yes, I saw Mrs. Preston, mamma, only I completely forgot her name when church was out, but I just turned around and talked hard, and I don't think she noticed in the least that I didn't speak it. I knew her at once, because she was so sweetly gowned. There were three other ladies in the seat behind us, but they were all strangers. There seemed to be lots of strangers there to-day; we had a man in our own pew. I told her all you said, and put in a nice little compliment about her being so fond of music, though I couldn't quite remember whether you said that or not, but it pleased her awfully for I saw her cheeks get as pink as roses. She said it didn't matter in the least about the invitation and she would be so glad to come, so now you needn't worry another bit about that lazy Miss Faulkes. I would dismiss her if I were you."

"Did you get Mrs. Preston's address, Celia?" asked the mother from her luxurious couch; "you know I must call upon her if possible before the *musicale*. She is a stranger and a new-comer, and I wish to show her some attention on account of her father knowing your grandfather so well."

"Yes, mamma, I did remember it, though it was just a

hairbreadth escape. I had to call her back to get it. You know I never can remember more than one thing at once; but really I deserve a good deal of credit, for I was dying to get over to the other side of the church to speak to Margaret Langdon before she got away. She is expecting her cousin home from Europe soon, you know, and I wanted to make sure he would be in time for Christobel's house party, because if he isn't I'm not going to accept, for there isn't another man going that I care a cent about except Ralph Jackson, and he's so overpoweringly engaged, there is no comfort for any other girl now in him. Let me see, where did I write that address."

The sweet voice tinkled on like the babbling of some useless little brook.

"Oh, here it is, mamma. Hazel Avenue—1515 Hazel Avenue. Say, mamma, isn't it rather queer for a Preston to live on Hazel Avenue? Are they poor? Her gown did not look like it. I should say it was imported. No one but a master-hand could have put those little touches to her costume."

Mrs. Lyman sat up regardless of the pillows that slipped to the floor.

"Hazel Avenue! Are you *sure*, Celia? You are so careless. Perhaps you have some other address mixed with it."

"No, mamma, I'm sure this time for I said it over after her, and I remember thinking it was a very dull part of town for that dress she wore to have come from."

"Celia, are you sure you got the right woman?"

"Sure, *perfectly* sure, mamma. I studied her sidewise during the closing hymn, for she didn't sit directly behind me. You said she had brown eyes and hair, and anyway, I remembered seeing her in the seat before. I'm sure it was the right woman. Now quiet down, mamma; if it had not been the right one she would surely have told me, wouldn't she? She was the perfect pink of refinement in manner and dress."

"Well, I suppose she would," said the mother, as her daughter rearranged the pillows for her, "but you are very careless for a girl of your age, and I shall have to call upon her to make sure it is all right. There is really no telling what you may have said to her, after all. And it does seem queer to invite some one from Hazel Avenue."

The house on Hazel Avenue which the Winthrops occupied had been just like all the rest on that street until three weeks before. One of Miriam's first moves toward a new way of living had been to have a conference with their landlord, the result of which had been that he agreed to make certain changes if she would make certain other changes. She had carefully considered and inquired the cost before she began and had put the matter in immediate operation so soon as she had the landlord's permission. A little carpenter work and painting, and some large panes of plate glass, and the house was transformed outwardly as well as inwardly. The neighbors regarded the curved bay window that occupied the place of the former two common windows with envy. A new front door and tiled vestibule had taken the place of their dingy predecessors, and a queer little odd-shaped window with leaded panes over the front door broke the straight, solemn line of the monotonous row, making an altogether pretty and dainty looking abiding-place.

The carpenter and painter had finished their work but the day before, and Miriam carefully arranged the filmy curtains and graceful palm branches, and was hovering over a newly filled window box in the second story curved bay window, which was aglow with bright blossoms and rich greenery, when she saw a carriage turn into Hazel Avenue from Fifteenth Street and stop before her door.

She did not wait to see who it was, but slipped to her bedroom, where lay on her bed a pretty house gown just finished, all but a few stray hooks which were waiting to be put on. It was the work of but a moment to slip into it, and she blessed the fates that had made her leave it there close at hand. She had tried it on but an hour before and so felt sure that it looked all right, and when her wondering but demure handmaid came to her door with the silver tray bearing Mrs. Lyman's card she found her mistress already fastening the waist of her gown and quite calm outwardly, although quaking inwardly. She was about to make her first entrance into real society, a genuine call from a society woman, and through no effort of her own. She rejoiced in that fact.

"Isn't it sweet here?" murmured Celia, who had begged to come along because she had fallen in love with the supposed Mrs. Preston.

"Very," said her mother with a relieved air, "quite modest and unassuming, but all that is required," and she settled back to await the coming of her hostess.

Miriam trembled as she crossed the little hall and wondered if she would be able to imitate the fashionable handclasp of the day which she had observed of late and had feared to attempt, but she came forward quite naturally in spite of her trepidation and welcomed her caller graciously. There was less assurance in Mrs. Lyman's manner than she had expected. In fact that lady seemed almost ill at ease as she rose to meet her, and she turned with relief to the fair-haired daughter, who immediately began to gush about the house which she called "sweet."

Mrs. Winthrop at once spoke of the kindness of Mrs. Lyman in inviting her to the *musicale*, expressing her delight in fine music, and an indescribable look came over Mrs. Lyman's face, while Miss Celia began to say something about all the Prestons being so fond of music, which her mother immediately drowned by plunging wildly into a conversation about something as far from music as she could think of.

It was a rather interesting call, altogether considered. The hostess felt herself to be on trial and was therefore not quite natural. The caller too was evidently somewhat distraught. Her daughter could scarcely wait until they were out at the carriage before asking her what was the matter. But Mrs. Lyman paused at the very threshold, a sudden thought reminding her that she did not know the name of this guest-to-be of hers.

"Is Mr.—that is, is your husband at home now?" She asked it hesitatingly, and Miriam, because of her tragic thought of her husband, felt herself flushing to the roots of her hair.

She made a great effort to control herself, for she knew she was blushing, but answered quietly enough:

"No. Mr. Winthrop has been obliged to go abroad on business. I am expecting him home soon."

"Ah, indeed. Then you must be lonely," murmured the caller, turning satisfied to go down the steps.

"Winthrop, Winthrop? Where have I heard that name? I know her face and I think I can recall his, but who are they? Celia, my child, into what have you led me?"

By this time the young lady had begun to suspect what was wrong, but she was not struck with the serious side. Instead she burst into a peal of laughter, whereat her mother laid a reproving hand upon her mouth.

"Hush, Celia, she will hear you," she said, and looked anxiously back at the little house fast vanishing from sight through the carriage window. "It really isn't so bad a house and she seems refined. I suppose it can't be helped now."

"And why should it?" said Miss Celia, sobering down. "She is perfectly lovely and had the sweetest little home. What does it matter who they are if they are nice, I would like to know? She looks as if she was perfectly happy. I should just enjoy such cozy love-in-a-cottage as that. I saw the dearest baby in white in the maid's arms up at that pretty window behind the flowers. I'm going to take her up. I don't care who she is and I don't see why you care. Aren't you 'who' enough yourself without bothering about other folks? It can't hurt you any, mamma, if her grandfather didn't know yours."

"Celia," said her mother severely, "you are very young and know very little of the world."

CHAPTER 6

•

The Campaign Opened

Altogether the day seemed slightly brighter to Miriam Winthrop than any that had preceded it since her trouble fell upon her. She had not failed at the first step. Marvelous help had come to her. It was a good omen. Unconsciously she took on a somewhat more cheerful attitude. It was not that the way was any less dark, but far ahead of her she thought she caught a glimmer of hope. It might fade as she approached, but it was there now and to it she would go.

She set her armor in array, and looking it over decided which bravery to wear to the *musicale*. Then as the shades of evening dulled the lustrous folds of silk and satin, she hung them all away and went to the nursery. She had been so weary that she had put aside her motherly duties often, and now she heard the baby's voice pleading for a story. Her heart pierced her that she had neglected her darling little one, and she came swiftly and took her from the nurse and in the old-time way snuggled the curly head in her arms and began to rock.

The baby looked up with a joyous smile and never a reproach.

"Oh, 'oo dear, pitty itty mommie. I so glad oo tummed. Sing me pitty song, mommie, sing poppie's song."

She almost stopped rocking, and a choking came into her throat. She could not sing that. It was a song she had woven out of her own happy heart when her first baby was in her arms, and night after night she would lull her

43

to sleep, their little Pearl, their oldest child, while Claude lay on the sofa nearby in the gloaming and listened, telling her it was the sweetest music earth could hold for him. The song had been sung to the other children and Claude had loved it until the children had come to call it "Papa's song." She thought of those happy, happy days, and the ray of hope that had dawned, vanished and left her in darkness once more. To think that he, after his devotion to her, could ever look like that into another woman's eyes! How could she take him back and forgive him, even if she succeeded in winning him once more to herself? It must be done for the children's sake and for the world's view, but how for her own heart's sake could there ever be any hope?

But the baby was pleading and the tears must be choked back. She would not grieve the little one unnecessarily.

"Mamma will sing 'Little Bo-Peep,'" she answered as brightly as her voice could compass.

"No, no; baby want poppie's song; mommie sing poppie's song." She was crying now, with her tender puckered little lips held up irresistibly sweet. How could she refuse? And after all, 'twas no harder than all the rest she must bear and do.

She caught her voice through the tears in her throat and began:

The birdies have tucked their heads under their
    wings
And nestled down closely, the dear little things
And my dear birdie is here in her nest,
With her head nestled close on her own mother's
    breast.

The wind whispers soft sleepy songs to the roses,
And kisses the buds on the tips of their noses;
Shall I sing a sleepy song soft to my sweet,
And kiss the pink toes on her dainty wee feet?

The butterflies folded their silver gauze wings,
And now sweetly sleep with all fluttering things.

Will you fold your paddies, my dear little girl,
And rest your tired footies, my precious wee pearl?

The violet's closed its pretty blue eye
That has gazed all day long at the clear summer sky,
Now droop the dark lashes over your eyes,
They are weary with holding great looks of surprise.

The flower bells have dropped their tired little heads,
And laid themselves down in their soft mossy beds,
Your golden head droops and your eyes are shut
   tight,
Shall I lay you down sweet on your pillow so white?

She crooned the song to a little tune that had woven
itself out of the years of her singing it, and seemed to fit
the words as no other melody could do, and the sleepy
little child in her arms nestled closer and closer, folding
her hands and closing her eyes as the song went on,
until with the last words the soft regular breathing told
the mother the baby was truly asleep. Still she sat and
held her, humming the melody, not daring to stop so
soon lest she should waken, and trying to make real
again the dear days when she had sat happily and sung
thus. But the dark rolling of deep waters was between
her and her husband, and a darker and more awful roll
of trouble separated them still farther from one another.

The other two children, sitting in the wide window
seat, had dropped their books as the light faded too
much for them to see, and sat listening to the song. Pearl
crept to her mother's side, slipped her soft little hand
inside her mother's and laid her head against her lap.

"Oh, mamma," said Carroll from the window in a
whisper that tried to be soft for the baby's sake, "when
will our father come back? It seems as if he had been
gone for years. Will he ever come back?"

And the poor mother's heart echoed the yearning cry,
"Will he ever come back?"

The days that followed were filled with toil, and plans
developed rapidly now, for hourly Miriam was growing
wiser in the ways of the world. The *musicale* was a great
help to her, for while she knew few present and kept

herself unobtrusively in the background, she had good opportunity to take notes. Mentally she went over her first list for her own teas and marked off some and put down others. She began to see possibilities of asking many of these others. The young girl, Celia, fluttered over to her and introduced her here and there, and with an enthusiasm characteristic of a young girl expressed her intention of coming to see the baby. Before she drifted away she had made an early appointment to call on Baby Celia, being delighted that they bore the same name. As Miriam Winthrop watched her move gracefully from this group to that and smile and say a pleasant word she saw the possibility of help in that girl and resolved to follow it up.

The days that followed the *musicale* opened up a new world for Miriam Winthrop. She began to grow in the good graces of many people whom she might not have met if she had not first been invited to the Lymans'.

Meantime letters from her husband announced positively that he would be at home at a certain time, now very near at hand, and Miriam in all haste gathered her forces and went over her visiting list. The list was very different now from the one she had first made out in her ignorance. Only one name had she blindly clung to throughout, which strict adherence to society etiquette would have ruled out for the present, at least, because of her being an entire stranger, and that was the name of the woman who headed her list. Just why she wanted her there she herself could not understand, but she felt as if she must meet her to begin the battle. With fearful heart and strong purpose that never once wavered, she sent out her cards. There would be plenty of time for her husband to understand the new state of things after he reached home and no possibility of his upsetting her plans if the invitations were already out when he returned. The fashion magazine had made it plain that her husband must be in evidence. Her own heart made it plainer that he must witness the fray from beginning to end if he was to be won over.

The invitations out, she set about her preparations for the day, which in general had been made long ago, but which she now planned out in every minute detail, so that the domestic wheels should move smoothly without the possibility of a hitch at the trying time.

She invited Miss Lyman and one or two other young people to lunch informally and practised on them without their knowledge. She sent the maid with Pearl to a child's party and bade her keep her eyes and ears open. The maid returned demure and said little, but showed that she had learned several lessons. Miriam began to feel that she could afford to rest and store up strength for the day of the first reception, when a new anxiety arose. Another letter from her husband announced that he would be delayed several days later than he had supposed and would now reach home on the day, the *very day*, of her first tea. What if he should be delayed? What if he should not come until afterward? How miserably she had planned! How her work would all be for naught! She foresaw in a flash the dreary anxiety of the day, of awaiting his arrival till the hour, of the having to dress and meet the people with her mind upon his arrival. And then what would he think? He might be angry to come home and find the house full of guests. There was no telling in these days what attitude he might take toward her. She drew a sigh of relief as she remembered that whatever he felt toward her he would veil till their guests were gone.

Just as she had foreseen it came to pass.

The simple flower decorations were all in place just where they would look the most natural and effective, the rooms were in perfect readiness for the guests. The maid attired in black with cap and cuffs and apron, the children disposed of in quietness for the afternoon, the refreshments at hand and the hostess exquisitely gowned.

And yet Claude Winthrop had not arrived. His wife looked anxiously from the window now and again. She had fortunately forgotten to wonder what he would say to the changed appearance of the outside of the house. She was only anxious to get him upstairs and ready for the company. She surveyed herself in a full-length mirror. Her cheeks were flushed with the unusual excitement, and her eyes almost feverishly bright. The gown was becoming, fitted her perfectly, and was worn with an air of perfect ease that did not convey the idea of its being an unusual thing for the wearer to be thus dressed. It may have been the one great absorbing thought that kept all others out, that made this possible, for she was naturally a timid woman, shrinking into herself and becoming painfully self-conscious at times in the presence of strangers. But love had transformed her into another being for the time. Not all the worldly wisdom of society, nor all the habits of generations could present a better front than this simple, unassuming ease which love and a question of life and death had made it possible for her to wear.

She glanced at her watch. Five minutes to the hour. She must be ready now. Some one might come at any minute. What if no one should come! For a moment she stood still at the thought of such dumb defeat. But no! She must not think of such a thing. Time enough for that trouble if it should come. She must go down and see if the rooms were just right. With haste she laid out her husband's clothes on the bed in the nursery, and gave orders that he be told at once where to find them when he came in. Then she heard the sound of carriage wheels and in a panic lest he had come, and she would have to face him with all that was unspoken in her heart, she fled to the parlor.

It was only Celia Lyman, who had promised to help her pour tea, and who had arrived early and chattered gleefully. She was young yet and looked at everything in a delightfully childish manner. She condoled with her hostess over the absence of her husband, and said ten times that he would be sure to get there soon, and she fluttered from one corner to another and called the rooms "perfectly fine" and "dear," and a hundred other adjectives her enthusiastic heart suggested, and told Miriam that she looked as sweet as a girl and that her husband would "just have to kiss her" when he got there, right before them all, she was so beautiful. Miriam's cheeks glowed for an instant over this approval. She cared not a straw whether Celia Lyman admired her, but she cared with her whole soul what her husband thought of her. In fact, she had come to feel that the whole matter depended largely upon the first impression, and now she began to think that it was a good thing he should have arrived too late for them to have any talk over the matter. The transformation would thus be greater—if only he came in time to see it at all.

The callers began to drop in by ones and twos. They really came. Miriam found herself wondering why they had cared to come and if they were surprised that she had dared ask them, but they seemed quite pleased and decorously unsurprised over the lovely spot when they got there. They lingered too, and declared she had been unkind not to have let them come before, and numerous pretty compliments. There was plenty to be done. Miriam was not used to the position of hostess. It taxed her brain to keep track of her guests and she felt that she ought to have given more attention to this one and that. She almost forgot about her husband's non-appearance for a few minutes, until the maid approached and said in low tones:

"Mr. Winthrop is here, ma'am, and says he will be down in a few minutes."

After that her heart thumped painfully and all sorts of questions began to bestir themselves. How had he taken it? What would he think of her and the house, and the people? She cast a hurried glance about and felt satisfied with those who had come. There were others—there was one other—who had not yet arrived, who might come—ah! She caught her breath with one of those quick sighs that told of high tension in the nerves and which had become habitual with her of late. Ah! then would come the crucial moment!

At that instant an elegant carriage had stopped before the door, a coachman and footman in livery mounting guard. The footman opened the carriage door, and altogether overawed the demure maid at the door whose education had not as yet included footmen, and a tall and beautiful woman in costly apparel stepped curiously into the house.

CHAPTER 7

•

A Challenge to the Enemy

The hostess had been trembling but a moment before at
thought of the possibilities of the next few minutes. But
when the arrival paused in the doorway of the pretty
reception room with eyebrows slightly uplifted, and
glanced about superciliously as if to take in the entire
situation, new strength seemed to come to her. All the
puzzling questions that had troubled her for the past
week vanished. She forgot that the woman who was entering the room was an entire stranger to her, that she
had dared to invite her without introduction or the
usual formalities of calling. Her mind bravely rose above
the thought of broken laws of etiquette and ignored everything but the mere fact that the woman was here, in
spite of it all. What motives had brought her were not her
concern now. That she had chosen to come to the house
of an obscure stranger was enough. There might be,
there doubtless were, curiosity, condescension, amusement—and worst of all, an interest in the house of
Winthrop—mingled together as an incentive. Nevertheless she had accepted the challenge and was here.

As though she had been all her life accustomed to
such functions the hostess calmly finished her sentence
to the fine, erect, white-haired old lady of undoubted
respectability to whom she was talking. It was a satisfaction to her afterward that Mrs. Sylvester had entered
just at the moment when Mrs. Carroll stood by her side.
The visitor would see that her other friends were not
altogether unknown.

Then glancing up as though she had just become aware of the new arrival, she came forward a step to greet her, unconsciously assuming a graceful, condescending manner. She wondered why her heart did not palpitate and why stumbling apologies did not frame themselves on her lips. But no! she seemed not to be herself.

"So glad you could come," she said graciously, and quite as if she had been saying those things for half a century, and not a hint of what was running through her mind, "I wonder *why* you came? I wonder why you *came*?"

The caller viewed the hostess as Goliath might have looked at David, and so well was the rôle assumed that she could not decide whether Mrs. Winthrop was wholly innocent or wholly subtle.

Others arrived just then. Mrs. Winthrop was obliged to turn to greet them. Therefore she was enabled to turn away without being either embarrassed or effusive. Mrs. Sylvester drifted a little farther away speaking to one or two whom she knew slightly. As a whole the assembled company were not intimates of Mrs. Sylvester's. She still wore a half-amused, half-curious expression, and kept her eyes fixed upon the hostess, even while talking with others. She studied her face, the becoming arrangement of the soft hair on the shapely head, then the dress, and a look of surprise grew in her eyes.

All these expressions were noted by another onlooker who had not yet entered the room.

Claude Winthrop had stopped before his own door and looked up at the house in bewilderment. What had happened since he left? The street was surely the right one. He glanced across to make sure. Yes, there were the familiar landmarks. Had Miriam moved away? Strange. Then the door was opened by the demure Jane in garb of black with immaculate linen, the insignia of her office, who explained in low tones that Mrs. Winthrop had some guests and would be glad if he would dress and come down as soon as possible. He would find everything prepared for him in the nursery.

With a hasty vision of elegant bonnets and silken

robes he slipped quickly through to the back stairs, and went up to the nursery in no pleasant frame of mind. What could all this mean? It was very careless of Miriam to have such a state of things going on when he arrived, and after so long an absence. It was not like a loving wife to be so thoughtless. He was weary too, and what kind of people were downstairs? A lot of relatives of hers perhaps. He would just let them understand that for the present it would be more convenient for them to postpone any further visits. He had come home and wanted his house to himself, and a chance to rest. These and like ill-natured thoughts passed through his mind while he impatiently went through the details of his toilet. But who could the people below stairs be? They wore bonnets many of them. It must be they were not here to stay. What in the world could it all mean? He was baffled in any attempt to answer his own questions. He grew angrier as his toilet progressed. He half resolved not to go down. It would serve his wife right for not coming to meet him. This had been what she had feared he would do. But his curiosity, as much as anything else, made him go down. He came in from the back hall, that he might view the room before entering. His first glimpse showed him rooms quite unfamiliar in arrangement, and filled with well-dressed, well-bred people who were chatting pleasantly and sipping cups of tea. Over in the center, near the front of the house, he caught a glimpse of a beautiful woman. The oval of her face seemed familiar and reminded him strangely of something he had once loved. She was exquisitely dressed in a gown all gray and shining with soft touches of sunset pink about it, that recalled the rose-hue in her cheek. He was glad that he was well dressed himself. Who could that woman be? A dart of memory brought a shaded lane with wild roses growing on either hand, roses the color of that soft pink stuff in the front of her gown, and the flush on the oval cheek—and Miriam turned her face to the front and raised her eyes, bright with excitement, for the moment deep with the brilliancy they had worn long ago on that summer evening in the lane of sweetbrier. Her husband's heart stood still.

Was that Miriam, or was it some wraith of his bewildered vision? That beautiful woman his wife? Strange he had forgotten, during his absence, how lovely she was. It was worth while going away to come home to such enchantment. How lovely, how graceful, how perfectly gowned! Oh, the joy of his young love returned to him! With one heart's throb he was a youth again and Miriam more beautiful than ever before him. He stood entranced in the doorway of his own parlor, gazing at his own wife.

And then what evil spell was this that brought a memory of the times when he had forgotten her? Who was that? Could it be? He rubbed his eyes. Mrs. Sylvester! In his home! In *their* home! The thought of her was repugnant to him just now, for his heart had been recalled to the days of simple joys and innocent love. Her haughty, supercilious bearing, her lofty, commanding smile, so familiar, were suddenly grown hateful. He saw her look at his wife—*his wife!* What did she mean by that amused, quizzical expression? She was not worthy to touch so much as a finger of his spotless Miriam, and yet—there came his wife forward to greet her. He caught his breath and was conscious that he was glad she paid no further homage to that guest than a mere greeting. His brows contracted angrily. It was not pleasant to think that he had paid sweet compliments to Mrs. Sylvester. He would rather forget that part now. What a fool he had been! He distinctly remembered that he had considered her beautiful. So she was, with a certain style of beauty, but—compare her with that flower-like loveliness of his wife! Two sides of his nature were fighting in the man's heart. He did not wish to meet that other woman now. He would wipe out some experiences of the past from his mind. Mrs. Sylvester had been well enough to while away an idle moment with, but why had he ever wished to leave Miriam's side?

But these thoughts went like flashes through his mind as he watched. A moment after a group standing close to the door turned and recognizing him drew him at once into the room, and he began making his way toward his wife, for he had a sudden longing to be near her—to protect her from the woman whose friend he had been glad to count himself but a little while before.

He spoke to this and that one, answering questions with little knowledge of what he said, his eyes always as much as possible, like Mrs. Sylvester's, upon his wife. People looked after him and noticed his gaze, and murmured, "How fond he is of his wife! A most charming couple," and then dropped back to themselves and their own petty themes.

He had almost reached his wife's side now. He could see the fine tendrils of hair as it waved up from her neck, just as he used to admire it long ago. How was it that he had not noticed her beauty lately? Was it all because of his little while away from her? There was but a divan between him and his wife now. He could reach over and touch her arm. He could see the texture of her gown and see the crystal of her clear eyes.

And then she turned, just in front of him, to speak once more to Mrs. Sylvester.

"It is good of you to be so unconventional as to come to us," she said brightly. "You have been so kind to my husband. He did enjoy his drive with you so much the other day. Do let me give you another lump of sugar in your tea? Miss Lyman, have you the sugar there?"

It was the inspiration of the moment. Just what, in her desperation, she hoped to accomplish, she was hardly sure herself. She did not know that her husband was within hearing, though she had seen him coming toward her a few moments before, and her heart had stood still, knowing that the next few minutes would tell much for or against her cause.

Miriam was perfectly at her ease. She wondered at herself as she heard the words that dared come to her lips, and knew that a smile was upon her face whose import was not felt in her cold, frightened heart. She chatted on brightly.

Mrs. Sylvester was nonplussed. How did Mrs. Winthrop learn about the drive? Had her husband been giving his own version to prevent trouble? Was she so very innocent, or was it consummate skill? She regarded

her hostess critically. Claude Winthrop, standing just behind and a little to one side, felt angered by her expression.

Just then she turned, saw him, and came forward, still
with the same curious expression on her face, regarding
him half-quizzically.

"Ah, Sir Claude," she said, her eyes lighting with a
new interest.

At the sound of her husband's name spoken so familiarly, Miriam also turned and saw him, and then facing
her guest and opponent flashed one look, a challenge to
the enemy. It was but an instant that the clear eyes
looked into the hard, unscrupulous ones, but the other
understood. With a half-amused smile still upon her
face she accepted the challenge, and Miriam moved
quickly to greet a caller, a silver-haired gentleman of distinction to whom she talked eagerly, thinking the while
how he had weathered the storms of youth and was
coming near the end of the toilsome journey, and she
searched in his face for some trace of peace at the
thought of victory.

The little by-play between the two women would not
have been noticed by an observer. Only they two understood. Claude Winthrop, looking on with disturbed
mien, comprehended only vaguely. He greeted Mrs.
Sylvester coldly, suddenly aware that his own wife had
met him after weeks of absence without so much as a
look of greeting.

His eyes followed her as she moved toward the man
with white hair, and his face grew rigid as he saw her
eagerly talking with him. He knew the handsome old
face crowned with the silver of honor to be but the white
sepulchre covering of a reprobate, a man without a conscience, who had no scruples whatever against satisfy-
ing his selfish nature. This was the weary, sainted
pilgrim to whom his wife thought she was talking. He
wondered once more over this strange gathering. How
came these people here? Where did Miriam get to know
them all? The scoundrel was a man of influence and reputation, not easily secured outside certain circles of so-

ciety, because though he was bad, he was also rich, influential, graceful in society, and withal knew how to ingratiate himself into the favor of women.

Claude Winthrop was suddenly recalled to himself by the voice of Mrs. Sylvester.

"I wish you would tell me what it is all for," she said playfully.

"I beg your pardon?" he said coldly, not understanding.

"Why all this?" answered the lady, waving her hand toward the roomful of people. "Why did you make her do it? Were you not satisfied with things as they were?"

"I do not understand you," he said, beginning to feel with rising anger that perhaps he did.

"How exceedingly obtuse you are this afternoon, Claude," she replied, laughing lightly and touching his sleeve with the tip of her fan as she darted a glance at Miriam, who seemed not to see it, but turned her deep eyes up to the white hair and gold spectacles, her face fairly glowing with a pleasure in his company which she did not feel. Instinctively she knew she must not seem to care.

Claude Winthrop drew back slightly at sound of his name. He felt a shame creeping into his face at thought of the pride he had felt when she had first called him thus. What had happened that had made things so different? How far had he gone? What a fool he had been! Did Miriam suspect? And how did Miriam know about that ride?

"Where have you been all this time, Claude?" said Mrs. Sylvester in her pleasantest tone. "You have not been near me for ages. I actually accepted your wife's invitation this afternoon to hunt you up. I have sent two or three notes and invitations to your usual city address but have heard nothing from you. I suppose she found you out from the fact that she knows about the ride. Poor boy, won't she let you have a little innocent amusement?"

Her tone had in it that caressing quality with which she had first subdued him to her feet. Its spell might have worked fully once more had it not been for that contemptuous, covert sneer as she spoke of his wife. His beautiful wife! He glanced over again at Miriam.

"Oh, she won't hear us; she's thoroughly engaged with Senator Bradenburg. She certainly cannot object so long as she amuses herself with such as he."

A certain shame rolled over him that he did not have the courage to knock this woman down for speaking in such terms of his wife, or at least to condemn her with words, as she was a woman and could not for that reason be knocked down. But he was silenced by the thought that he had given her ground for speech of this kind. Had he not dishonored Miriam by admiring this woman, another man's wife, nay by visiting her often and making sweetly turned speeches to her, amusing himself by writing bits of poems about her eyes, likening them to all the stars and jewels of the universe, when his own Miriam's eyes held depths unknown to Mrs. Sylvester? For very shame's sake his tongue was tied.

"I have been abroad for eight weeks," he replied weakly, and instantly saw that he was making apologies for not having been to see Mrs. Sylvester. Also he knew that he had felt called upon to make this apology, and he further added: "I have not yet been to the city office, as I just returned to-day, and therefore I suppose the mail you sent there is still awaiting me."

Then he could have kicked himself for having made the explanation as he saw the light come into Mrs. Sylvester's eyes.

"Truly I am glad there is some such reason. I thought you had grown weary of—" she paused and added "us." Then she laughed lightly and looked into his face as if to make it plain that she meant herself by the pronoun.

To Claude Winthrop this intimacy had suddenly become hateful. He longed for courage to tell the woman by his side so, but his dissembling heart said, "Wait, treat her pleasantly and show her that you have meant nothing by your former actions but mere friendship. You can gradually make her see that you love your own wife."

But even as he thought this, the memory of a certain

night—when, as it seemed to him now, he must have lost his senses, he had bent over the woman beside him and kissed her lips, letting his arm linger about her waist as he did so—brought the waves of red blood over his face.

He had not gone long or far in the treacherous way or he would not so suddenly have been brought to see himself in this light. The absence from home, the changed aspect of everything, Miriam's beautiful appearance and the contrast between these two women brought thus unexpectedly together before him had combined to effect it. And yet he had not the courage to do anything. He despised himself even while he answered Mrs. Sylvester's low-spoken questions in a distraught way. He was thankful when she made her adieus, and was only half aware that his last word had been a promise to come to her home the next evening.

CHAPTER 8

•

New Views of Things

'Tis not to cry God mercy, or sit
   And droop, or to confess that thou hast failed;
'Tis to bewail the sins thou didst commit,
   And not commit those sins thou hast bewailed.
He that bewails and not forsakes them too,
   Confesses rather what he means to do.
                    —*Francis Quarles.*

Claude Winthrop noticed with relief as he turned back to the parlor that most of the guests had departed. He would now get a chance to speak to Miriam. And yet he was not half so sure that he wished to see her alone as he had been a little while before. Her mention of that ride of his with Mrs. Sylvester had made him uneasy in her presence. How much did she know? How did she know anything?

He was almost relieved to find that the end was not yet, and that Miss Lyman and a friend of hers were to remain to dinner. His wife took no more notice of him than if she had seen him but the hour before and arranged the whole programme with him. Indeed, now that he began to observe carefully he saw that she skillfully avoided saying anything to him except in the most general way.

He began to notice the changes in the rooms. How exquisitely everything was arranged! What a difference had been made. How had it been accomplished? All these years with Miriam he had not known that she possessed such capabilities. There positively had been nothing that even Mrs. Sylvester could have sneered at,

though of course there was not such a display of wealth
as one beheld in her house. But everything was in keeping. It did not suggest unlimited income, but it must
have cost something and where had the money come
from? He frowned and wondered if Miriam had been
running into debt. But a glance at her graceful form
made him forget possible bills.

With the inconsistency of a man who has long in-
dulged himself in selfishness he forgot that he had been
anxious to see Miriam during the whole latter part of his
journey that he might find fault with her for not answering some of his important business questions, and indeed for not writing him at all during his absence. He
had gone about so much that at first he had not noticed
it, laying it to failure of mails, but as the time drew near
to get home and some business questions still remained
unanswered he began to feel the grievance of her un-
wifely action. He had intended giving her a sound going
over for allowing him to be so anxious concerning her
health and the children's all that time, and he actually
thought, poor blind fellow, that he had been anxious
about her, even while he was preparing some wounding
sentences for her ear on the subject.

But now as he sat at his own well-appointed table with
the sort of guests about it he had always craved, and his
beautiful wife opposite, he told himself that he had been
eager for days to see her once more, to have her to himself, and here he was being kept from her for hours by
strangers. He forgot Mrs. Sylvester for a time, forgot everything save the latest impressions of his wife. He
watched her constantly and admiringly, comparing her
favorably with a certain famous actress he had seen in
Paris. There was something fresh and unsullied about
the purity of his wife's face that reached his better self
and touched the feelings that had first attracted him to
her. Some men need always to have their best joys kept
constantly at a distance in order that they may appreci-
ate them at anything like their full value.

Claude Winthrop began to grow anxious for the dinner guests to depart, and turned from the door as he

bade them good evening with a sigh of relief and anticipation.

He turned, intending to clasp his wife in his arms. He
expected to find her blushing shyly and smiling behind
him, as had been her wont in their early married days
when guests had broken in upon their close companionship. But he found empty air behind him. He took a
step forward into the little reception room, thinking she
had coyly stepped in there lest some lingering servant
should witness their glad meeting. But she was not
there. He peered into the little music room beyond, and
came back into the hall blankly looking for her. Above,
in the distance he heard the cry of a child and the quick
stir of rustling, and then a door closed, and subdued
voices murmured at intervals.

He called but there came no answer, until he called
again. He was becoming angry. It was no way to treat him
on his home-coming. Other women did not treat their
husbands so—at least other women did not treat him
coldly. He was about to mount the stairs when the maid
appeared at the head of the stairs, and said, in a low tone,
that Mrs. Winthrop had been obliged to go to the baby
who had cried for her.

He frowned slightly that she was delayed again, but
doubtless the guests had kept her from the baby a long
time and she would soon be able to soothe Celia to sleep
and would come to him. He stepped back to the parlor
and looked about him. Miriam certainly had good taste.
He walked from one end of the room to the other,
touched a cushion here, smoothed the broad cool leaf of
a palm that stood near him and then glancing down, a
prism of light caught his eye. He stooped and picked up
the glittering object. It was a slender hoop of jewels, and
as he looked at it there seemed something familiar about
the setting of it. Where had he seen it before? Ah! it was
Mrs. Sylvester's, for he had seen it upon her wrist again
and again. He could seem to remember its gleam in his
eyes as he came to himself after that guilty kiss. A coldness came into his fingers, a horror at himself and the
shadow of wrong that he was beginning to realize in his

life. He dropped the bracelet from his nerveless fingers, and then as quickly picked it up. Miriam must not see it. It seemed to him the pretty jeweled thing would tell his secrets to her by the light of its piercing gems that could reveal only the truth. He turned the bracelet over and saw engraved initials inside, S. S. for Sylvia Sylvester from—those were Senator Bradenberg's initials, but of course it was not likely; still—and a feeling of loathing came over him for the woman in whose company he had stood in that very spot but three hours before. With sudden resolve he hid the bracelet in his inner pocket. Miriam must not see it. He must return it. He saw at once that the call he promised would have to be made. It never occurred to him that it would be decidedly better for Miriam to send the bracelet herself. He dreaded to speak to her of that other woman, and how else would Miriam know to whom the bauble belonged? How indeed! and what would she think of him for knowing so exactly to whom it belonged with only initials to guide him?

He sat down to wait for Miriam, resting his head against the sharp back of a chair and feeling as if the bracelet pressed against his heart and hurt it as the chair did his head.

Upstairs he could hear a low murmur of a lullaby interspersed with the wail of a baby in protest. The soft tapping of a trotting foot came regularly. This went on for a long time. Claude Winthrop was impatient. He had waited already long enough.

A last the maid came downstairs.

"Mrs. Winthrop says please not to wait for her. Little Miss Celia is not well and she must stay by her," she said with respectful tone, and was gone. He remembered afterward that she had been carrying a hot-water bottle. The baby must be unusually out of sorts. He yawned impatiently and went upstairs to his room. It certainly was very awkward and disagreeable in Miriam not to give him a chance to even kiss her on his return. She might have slipped away from the baby for a minute. But no, women always thought of their children first before their husbands. It made no difference how much they slighted the one whom they had professed to love above every other earthly creature, if only a baby cried. It was the old grievance he had had before he went abroad. By use of it he managed to forget the bracelet and its uncomfortable reminders for a little while.

Before he undressed he listened at the door. All seemed quiet in the hall. He tiptoed softly toward the nursery door. The light was turned down and only the rays from the street electric light outside showed the dim outline of his wife sitting at the farther end of the room. She had slipped off the reception gown and wore a soft loose pink garment with little frills of white. In the dusk it took on the softness of a cloud at evening. The little curly head nestled in the hollow of her arm gave the touch of a madonna to the picture. Miriam's head was turned away. He could only see the profile, against the flaring light outside, sweet and pure and sad. What had she to be sad about? His ever-ready anger rose, even while his conscience reproached him. Yes, she was lovely. She was lovelier even than in the promise of her youth when he had first loved her. He would go in softly and stoop over and kiss her as he used to do long ago, so softly that the sleeping baby would not wake, kiss that sad look away and bring her lovely loving smile. He half made a movement to start and then the baby stirred and gave a hoarse cry. He recognized at once the croupy cough, and saw Miriam's strong white hands move quickly as she replaced the cold wet compress from a dish of water at her side.

The maid was coming too with hot water to make steam in the room. It was an all-night job he knew at once. But it was not serious. He could see that already the worst barking roughness of the cough was checked. They knew what to do and he was better out of the way. He tiptoed silently back to his room and closed the door just as the maid reached the top landing of the stairs. It was just as well for him to go to bed at once. Miriam could not get away.

And Miriam sat the long night through and thought. Even after the baby was breathing naturally again and tucked in her little warm crib, and could as well have been left to the experienced nurse, she sat with her head bent over the rail of the crib and did not sleep.

The die had been cast. She had made her first entrance into society! And it had not been altogether a failure, though she was not sure how much of a success it had been. Time only could tell that.

She forced herself to go over the details of the afternoon and evening. She felt again her heart freeze at sight of the graceful, dreadful woman who entered her home in bodily presence—who had entered it in spirit as a serpent sometime before. She shrank once more from meeting her husband's gaze. She knew she had not done so yet. She wondered if he knew it. She had felt the surprise in his face ever since he had come. She knew that he was pleased with her appearance and the house. She recognized a change of tone toward herself. She might if she chose be on a more intimate footing now than she had been for some months back. The coldness and harshness that had characterized him were gone. That she knew intuitively. So far she had scored a point. Her longing, loving heart had told her this even without looking him clearly in the eyes. But the great gulf that was fixed between their hearts was kept there at her command, not his, now. He might be willing to bridge it, for a while at least—her heart winced as she bravely added that last clause; but for her it could never be bridged until all possibility of his ever crossing it away from her again was removed, if it ever could be removed.

She wondered at herself that could love and yearn, and long to lay her sick child down and go to him and lay her head upon his breast and tell all her aching heart-full to him and let him comfort her as he used to do; and this while she knew that his friendship with that graceful, unprincipled woman with the steel eyes was as yet unreckoned for. And yet her pride and her poor hurt love would never let her yield to all her yearnings till the fight was fought clear through to the end and she had won, if win she might. And she was weary, weary unto death, she thought. Life looked very black at best. What good was she to accomplish by all this worldly panorama in which she had become a puppet? And then her aching heart cried out against the husband who could be so weak as to bring all this suffering and distress upon her he had professed to love. What was love anyway but a passing phase of the emotions? She thought with a shudder of a bit of rhyme; where had she read it? a scrap at the head of a chapter of some book. It had grated on her when she read it, and she had thought with pity of the one who would write it, and contrasted his circumstances with hers. That had not been her happy experience of love, but that was before—

> Oh, love's but a dance,
>   Where Time plays the fiddle!
> See the couples advance,
>   Oh, love's but a dance!
> A whisper, a glance—
>   "Shall we twirl down the middle?"
> Oh, love's but a dance,
>   Where Time plays the fiddle!

Was it true? Was love but that? Was there nothing real nor lasting?

And then what strange absurdity of the mind brought back the text of that sermon she had heard, the only sermon or text she seemed ever to have heard in her life as she thought of it now: "See that thou make all things according to the pattern shewed to thee in the mount."

If one did things according to that pattern, would it make a difference? Would love be true while life lasted?

And at last with the burden of all she must do pressing heavily upon her, and with the dread of the morrow and what it might bring forth hanging over her, she fell asleep, one hand upon the baby's hand and her cheek resting uncomfortably on a little flannel double-gown folded against the crib rail.

CHAPTER 9

•

At Mrs. Sylvester's

Was she a maid, or an evil dream?
Her eyes began to glitter and gleam;
   He would have gone, but he stayed instead;
Green they gleamed as he looked in them:
"Give me my fee," she said.
                    —*Christina G. Rossetti.*

Miriam presided at the breakfast table the next morning
in an elaborate little morning robe the like of which she
had been wont to consider too fine for everyday use.
Now nothing was too good. All, all was put into her venture. She would exchange it for a simpler one as soon as
her husband was out of the house, meantime it had its
use.

On one thing she had forgotten to reckon. The children met her in the hall and began to exclaim joyously
on her appearance, but she hushed them before their
father heard. She did not care to reveal any of the ma-
chinery of her maneuver by having him suppose it was
unusual for her to be dressed in this way. If he noticed it,
well and good, but better not wear it than to have it remarked upon.

She had managed to put on with the dress her fine
distant manner of the evening before. Her husband felt
that the moment he entered the breakfast room. It
seemed like a sweet, far-off mist that enveloped her,
through which, try as he would, he could not break. She
looked a little pale after her night's vigil, but she had
chosen her gown with regard to her pallor, and so it but
made her the more interesting. A little while before she

66

would have despised herself for such small subterfuges, now they seemed all important.

She smiled behind the coffee cups over her night of watching and said she would be all right after a few hours' sleep, and then told her husband of a concert for which she had tickets that evening.

He looked surprised, but her manner was so assured, quite as if they had been going out in society for years together, that he said nothing, especially as the maid and the children were present. He was more puzzled than ever over the new order of things. Miriam mentioned the hour of the concert, and suggested that he be sure to come home early to dress for it.

The bracelet in his pocket suddenly recalled to him his half-engagement for the evening. He became somewhat abstracted and fell to wondering if he could possibly have the face to call at the Sylvester house and get rid of that annoying bit of jewelry as well as its owner before going to the concert. He tried to recall whether Mrs. Sylvester had said anything about afternoon tea. What day was it? Yes, she was always at home on that afternoon. He could call late, when others had gone, get the disagreeable business out of the way forever and then he could breathe freely and enjoy the concert with his wife.

He was so engrossed in these thoughts that he forgot to feel aggrieved when Miriam left the table before he was through on the excuse of going to Celia, and said as she paused at the door that she would lie down in her room for a couple of hours and she wished they would try not to disturb her.

She vanished and he had the memory of a pretty vision in the doorway. He had meant to see her alone for just a moment anyway before going downtown, but she was gone now and perhaps it was just as well. He would get the Sylvester matter out of the way before he kissed her and then he would feel his conscience clear. Old scores would be wiped out. He would take good care to warn Miriam against that woman. She was not fit company for her. Whatever possessed her to invite her? How did she ever meet her? Pondering, he came to feel quite as if his friendship with Mrs. Sylvester had been

through no fault of his own, but wholly owing to her
malign influence, to which in some hour of mental aber-
ration he had weakly yielded, scarcely realizing what
would be the outcome and so was not so very much to
blame after all. He would make a clean breast of it to
Miriam sometime and that would show her that she
must have nothing further to do with Mrs. Sylvester.

He finally managed to cajole his conscience into the
belief that all this sophistry was true and actually settled
to his morning paper with something like a pleasant anticipation of the evening. That Sylvester part would be
hard to get through with but he meant to do it, and it
was pleasant that he need not rebuke himself for keeping his promise to her. He was glad of that, for now he
had a real reason for going, a legitimate one.

And Miriam doffed the pretty gown and crept to her
couch in the darkened chamber with heavy sobs shaking her frame. She would not allow them to break into
the outburst of tears that would have relieved the tension. There would be traces of that on her face and she
could not afford to show any such emotion now. The
concert was a link in the chain. It was to be a great society affair, a brilliant performer and the last night. The
tickets had been held high and she had paid dearly for
the seats she had secured among the high and mighty
ones. She would not have been able to compass such
places at all, but for the opportune inability of some
friends of the Lymans who were called to a distant fu-
neral unexpectedly and could not use their own seats.
Celia Lyman had heard of it and eagerly offered to get
her the seats two days before. The concert was to be the
next movement in the plan of campaign, which now that
it was started seemed to grow of itself. Mrs. Sylvester
would be sure to be there. Miriam tried to think how she
must do and what she should wear for that evening, but
at last nature took her revenge and she fell asleep.

Claude Winthrop managed to get through a tolerable
toilet at his club—he had borne the call in mind when he
dressed that morning—and a little before six o'clock,
without having yet gone home, he rang the bell at the
Sylvesters'.

Mrs. Sylvester's footman had been accustomed to his calling frequently, often at this hour. Without announcing him in the reception room, where Claude could hear several voices and the clink of late tea things, he led him to a small reception room to the right of the doorway heavily hung with *portières*. He sent word that he would like to see Mrs. Sylvester immediately, if possible, for just a moment. In a few minutes he heard the soft rustle of her dress and her white hand drew back the heavy folds of drapery.

She came in with her most confidential air and a light of welcome in her eyes.

"So good of you to come the first possible minute," she said holding out both hands to greet him, "But let me tell you, Claude, I knew you would!"

There was assurance in her tone and a favor that stirred the lowest in him. He writhed inwardly. It was going to be very hard to do what he had planned to do. He could not broach the subject at once. He wished she would be a little reserved as she knew well how to be.

"You mistake," he said and tried to say it coldly, but somehow his voice sounded strange to himself, "I merely ran in on an errand. I cannot stay. I am due at home now. I promised to take my wife to the concert at the Academy."

"Oh, what a pity!" She said it sweetly, but there was a hardness under the surface tones and a sharp glitter came into her steel eyes. Her mouth always wore a determined look; the pretty curve of red set itself in thin lines of compression now.

"I must excuse myself from the others, then, and attend to you at once." She said it and was gone before he had time to demur. He was searching for that annoying bracelet. It would help to open the way for the further remarks he had to make, though now he was ready for them he could not think for his life what he had meant to say. Ah, there was the bracelet in his inner breast pocket. How annoying! She would think he had placed it over his heart on purpose. It was a bad beginning, but—and then he looked up and realized what she had said and that she was gone. He was angry and relieved all in one, angry that he had not got the matter done with while she was there without further delay, glad that he had time to think what to say. He wanted her to understand that he was sorry for his foolishness—say that he had been but playing, how would that sound? He could soften it by saying he knew she meant the same, and then a vision of Miriam looking at him with her clear eyes while he made his "clean breast" came and made him tremble. His throat grew dry and hot. He could hear Mrs. Sylvester's voice in the distance in farewells. He knew that sound, having waited for it more than once in this same room. She knew how to dismiss people in a way that sent them home thinking they had made the move to go themselves. She would soon get rid of them all. He heard the front door close and a pause, and low voices for a few minutes and then steps and the front door closed again. She did not come. He looked impatiently at his watch and felt feebly in his brain for suitable phrases to clothe his message.

At the farther end of Mrs. Sylvester's long reception room in the shelter of a window seat, sat Senator Bradenberg and Mrs. Sylvester. They were talking in low tones. There was about their manner a freedom as of two who understood each other fully. Each recognized the power of the other in certain directions. Each trusted the other because each was to a certain extent in the power of that other and knew it. This made the basis of a friendship that was not unpleasant, at times, when it suited the convenience of the two concerned. Each had about the same amount of unscrupulousness. They were well suited.

"I will do it," she said looking him straight in the eye, "if you will do something for me. It is about as pleasant as the task you have given me, so we are even again. You said a little while ago you would go to the concert tonight with me. Now I want you to go instead with Mrs. Winthrop. She is pretty and she is new. It will not be hard work. Never mind what my object is. Just be on hand a little before the appointed hour, and gracefully— as you well know how—make her understand that her husband was detained, and that you have come in his place. Stay. You may make it more complete. Say he will meet her at the concert to take her home. I will see that he is there. You understand how to do it perfectly. I need not tell you."

The silver head was bowed.

"Thank you," he said, touching his heart suggestively with his hand on which a rare diamond glittered, "and in return?"

Her hand was on the bell. She touched it and turned with a satisfied smile.

"In return I will invite your awkward, clumsy congressman to my house and endeavor to charm him long enough at least for you to get your precious vote taken."

She turned and spoke a word of command to the footman, and they rose and walked slowly up the length of the parlor, the white head bowed low once more, and this time he touched her hand with his lips, and she returned the salute with a playful little tap on his pink, wicked old cheek.

It was just as they had reached the door that Claude was ushered into the larger room by the footman. The senator understood at once. He shook hands graciously and declared he was glad to see Mr. Winthrop at home once more, that he was looking well, and he had enjoyed the few minutes spent yesterday in their delightful little home with his most charming wife for hostess.

Then he bowed himself out. He was a wise and wily old serpent.

Claude drew himself up. He knew Senator Bradenberg. All the men knew him. What was he doing here with Mrs. Sylvester? And that bracelet!—were those really his initials? Then he winced as he remembered that this was no concern of his now. He was not jealous for Mrs. Sylvester. What a contrary thing was human nature. It was Miriam for whom he was jealous. He did not want her pure name on lips so sullied—and he felt a soothing qualm of righteous wrath pass over him.

Mrs. Sylvester had given an order to the footman in a low tone.

"Now Claude," she said in her *tête-à-tête* tone of voice,

"I have kept you such an unconscionable time that you will not get home in time for dinner before the concert, so I have told Warner to have dinner served at once and we will go right out to the dining room, and you can talk while you eat. I am absolutely alone to-night. Mr. Sylvester is in Chicago for a week, perhaps longer, and Miss Page dines in her room. She complained of sick headache this afternoon." She did not add that Miss Page had been informed, but three minutes before, that her dinner would be served to her in her room.

Claude looked helplessly about him. It was late. There seemed no way out of this tangle into which he had inadvertently strayed. He had a wild thought of flinging the bracelet down and starting for the door, but instead he bit his lips and followed his voluble hostess into the brilliant dining room.

It was not a pleasant dinner. The guest was *distrait*. The hostess talked without interruption giving him details of a small scandal that had been enacted during his stay abroad, about which neither cared a whit.

Claude ate hurriedly, hoping to hasten the courses, and then waited impatiently for Mrs. Sylvester to finish. She seemed to be in no haste now that they were seated, and the courses came with unusual slowness for a well-regulated house. He glanced in dismay at the great carved clock as the silver chimes rang half-past seven, and shoved his chair back in alarm. What had he been about? Not a word of his errand had he spoken, and it was already too late to reach home in time to take his wife to the Academy at the time she had named.

He drew the bracelet out of his pocket and threw it down on the fine deep linen between them, but before he had time to explain Mrs. Sylvester had arisen and taken it quietly, as if she had expected it to be there. Long afterward he wondered if she had dropped it on purpose. But now he did not think of that as she quickly clasped it on her white arm. There was a determined look in the red cupid's line of her mouth and her eyes burned a cold blue flame, as if she knew she had come to a critical moment and meant to tide herself well over.

"Claude," she said, and coming over to his side she

placed the white hand on his arm, "you need not look so frightened. Just enjoy yourself. I have fixed it all right. Your wife is not expecting you. I sent her word some time ago that you were detained—you were, you know—and that entirely against your will," and she laughed a silvery laugh of assurance.

Claude had grown white around his mouth.

"You sent my wife word—" he said hoarsely trying to rise and shake that hateful pretty hand from his arm. He suddenly saw his crime in all its enormity. It was as if he saw it through Miriam's eyes.

"Yes, I did," she answered laughing, "and you need not look so frightened. It is all right and proper. You are to meet her at the Academy. I sent her a charming escort, who was delighted to be of service, and he has explained it all. By this time they are starting and very soon we will start too. Come, be a good boy, and talk to me while I finish my coffee."

CHAPTER 10

•

The Plot Thickens

"And what you leave," said Nell, "I'll take,
  And what you spurn, I'll wear;
For he's my lord for better or worse and worse,
  And him I love, Maude Clare.
Yea, though you're taller by the head,
  More wise and much more fair;
I'll love him 'till he loves me best,
  Me best of all, Maude Clare."
                    —*Christina G. Rossetti.*

Miriam had awakened from her long sleep to accomplish many things. The dinner which awaited her husband would have been much more enjoyable to him than the one which he tried to choke down at Mrs. Sylvester's. His wife had remembered his every like and dislike and the appointments of the table were exquisite. She had resolved that he should find no pleasanter place than his own home in so far as it was in her power. Therefore she took as much pains about the setting and decoration of the dinner table as she had done the night before when they were entertaining guests. It was hard to have to treat one's husband like a stranger, and she sighed as she remembered the cosy little suppers taken on the kitchen table on the girl's "day off," when she and Claude had not taken time to eat in a regular way but had brought the baby's high-chair out to the kitchen and she had ransacked the pantry and refrigerator for nice little tidbits and sent a savory smell forth from the gas-stove while Claude quoted a verse of Riley's poem, "When mother gets the supper," and the baby crowed over the delightful informality of the occasion as she drummed on a tin pan. But that was oh, so long ago! And now she was putting touches to the fern dish that had just come from the florist's little shop around the corner exactly as if Claude were an outsider.

The supper was perfectly cooked and was ready at the appointed hour. After that it stayed in a continual state of readiness until it had depreciated its value more than half and finally the cook declared sulkily that it was "intoirly spoiled." Then the children were given their dinner and sent off to bed, and Miriam took a few mouthfuls, her mind in such a state of uneasiness that she scarcely tasted what she ate. But she knew she must eat if she would go through the evening. What could have happened to Claude? Would he not come at all? Had he forgotten?

For the hundredth time she walked to the mirror to see that everything was right about her costume.

It was an exquisite creation of filmy black over clear white that she had chosen for the evening, which could not have been accomplished save by her skillful needle, without a vast outlay of money. She knew this, and again and again looked it over critically to be sure there was no mark of "home-made" about it, and again felt sure that no one would know it was not made by a master hand.

She put up her hand to her throat to still the choking sensation that would keep rising as the minutes flew by and her husband did not appear. She touched the string of pearls, a wedding gift, from a maiden aunt. She half smiled as she remembered the laughing prophecies made by her girl friends of a tear which she must shed for every pearl the bride wore. How sure she had been that they would not come true, how little fear of the old superstition! And yet she had shed tears enough, and about such petty things. So many that she had not any left now wherewith to water her first, her only, her awful sorrow when it did come!

Ah! that clock! The hands were painfully near to half-past seven. And Claude must eat his dinner, and the distance to the Academy was not short, and she so dreaded going late at this her first entrance into that charmed circle.

But hark! There was a carriage! And steps! Had Claude waited perhaps to get the carriage and come home in it that he might not have to keep her waiting so long! How good of him to think of it! She had not ventured a carriage. She had known the expense must be saved wherever possible if she would not run short in her venture into the world.

Why did he not come in quickly? She was so glad over the carriage that she forgot for the instant all that had gone before, and the reason for her cool demeanor toward her husband. It was so hard to play this distant unconcerned role toward one who had been a part of herself for so long.

Why, there was the bell! Claude had forgotten his latch-key perhaps, or lost it. She rushed forward to the door. There was no time to waste now. She laid grip upon her self-control and remembered she must not give way to her feelings as she put her hand upon the knob and then she opened the door to come face to face with—not Claude as she had expected, but the smiling face of the silver-haired senator.

Her cheeks had grown pink during the last half-hour with excitement. She was really a beautiful woman and she struck the senator so as he greeted her deferentially. He was glad he had come. The prospect before him was a pleasant one.

Miriam stood speechless for an instant, so sure had she been that it was Claude's step she heard. Then she recovered her self-possession and held out her hand in greeting. She was conscious of relief that the caller was an old man and would not therefore see through the disguise she would put over her uneasiness. But she liked the senator. All women did when he chose to have them do so. Her smile was genuine, though she wondered as she explained her acting as door maid, whether he would stay long, and whether Claude would not come soon. Also she was conscious of a disappointment about the carriage and realized how near she had been to forgiving Claude all just because of a paltry carriage and a little supposed thought of her convenience.

And then she became aware that Senator Bradenberg was not coming in, that he was trying to explain something to her.

"I have come in your husband's place to take you to the Academy," he was saying, "and I do hope, my dear madam, that you will let me do all in my power to make up for his loss. It is certainly a privilege to be allowed—"

Miriam in quick alarm put her hand on her heart, crushing as she did so some exquisite white rose buds that rested there among the lace.

"Has anything happened?" she said in a frightened voice. "Is Claude hurt?—or ill?"

The senator decided that she was a very beautiful woman and that he would not object to seeing her color come and go on his account like that. It would be worth working for.

"Oh, no indeed, Mrs. Winthrop," he said in his most suave manner. "Nothing is the matter at all. He was merely detained longer than—ah—he expected to be—and—ah—we made this little arrangement. He expects to meet you, I believe, at the Academy, when I suppose I shall unfortunately have to surrender in his favor. Meanwhile I am delighted to be so fortunate as to have your company, if you will permit, and the carriage is at the door."

With beating heart and eyes bright with tears that seemed scorching to get out, Miriam hastened to be ready. Her gloves and wraps were at hand. She had expected to have to hurry. But somehow this new move made things so hard. Where was Claude, and what could be the matter? Oh, was there to be some new, terrible revelation! Why had she started out on this fool's attempt to conquer what she did not know?

But she was glad it was Senator Bradenberg and not some younger man her husband had sent. She could talk politics to him and he would never notice how preoccupied she was. He was a good, kind man, old enough to be her father. And thanks to the hint in her magazine she had read enough of the questions of the day not to quake over the thought of a talk with even this noted man. There were subjects enough to talk about. She would ask him questions thick and fast and let him do the talking, that was the way to make people think you a good conversationalist, just be a good listener. But when would Claude appear, and how should she discover what had kept him? Would he tell her of his own free will? She must not forget again the manner she was maintaining toward him. If she once let him see that she was acting all would be lost.

How pleasant it was that she was to have the escort of so distinguished a man as the senator if she could not have Claude. It would surely give her prestige, for he seemed to be spoken of as a talented man who stood high in the political as well as the social world, and could command much influence.

Then she went down to her escort, ready, trying to smile and thanking him for being so kind as to come. She feared that she had not been so cordial as she might have been at first, she had been so taken aback.

"Where did you say you met Mr. Winthrop?" she asked as the carriage door slammed shut and they started on their way.

The senator cleared his throat and spoke with a pleasant unconcern. He was used to such situations. In fact he rather enjoyed them.

"At Mrs. Sylvester's. He was, I believe, on for a little dinner there and found it impossible to make both engagements fit, hence I am here. I do hope you won't find me a very great bore!"

"At Mrs. Sylvester's!" said Miriam and her voice sounded like death, even to herself. The carriage was passing a brilliantly lighted square and her white face was lit up for the moment. She turned piteous eyes of entreaty toward the senator as she spoke.

"You poor child!" said the senator in his graceful, caressing tone. "It is terribly disappointing to have one's husband off with another woman while you have to take up with any one that comes along, isn't it? but it is the way of the world, you know."

A flood of crimson concealed the pallor on Miriam's cheeks. There might be anything or nothing in these words, but instantly she was on the alert. Even an old man, old enough to be her father, should not see and pity. She had felt that he had meant pity for her, real pity in that sentence, though he was too polite to really say it, and had turned it off with pleasantry. But no one should suspect the torture she was passing through. Instantly summoning all her self-control she responded with a gayety that surprised herself:

"Not at all. I quite enjoy the prospect. I shall ask you a hundred and one questions whose answers I have been aching to know this long time, if you will not mind. Yes, of course, Claude is at Sylvesters'. I ought to have remembered—she is quite a friend of ours you know—didn't you see her at our house yesterday? I fear you thought me quite ungrateful, but I assure you I am only too delighted to have this opportunity of talking with you."

And then she summoned to her bidding all the reading she had been doing lately, all the talk of the daily papers about leagues and intrigues, all the confusing tangle of subjects that have two sides to them, and sometimes three sides, and began to ply her questions.

Senator Bradenberg watched her closely as well as he could do for the dim lights that flashed past as they rode. Here was certainly a marvelous woman, a woman worth cultivating. She was evidently acting. He was too well versed in the world not to know beyond a doubt the meaning of that tone when she had first said, "At Mrs. Sylvester's!" But how quickly she had rallied, what a beautiful color she had summoned to her aid. That he could detect beneath the mask of smiles a pain too deep for utterance, only added zest to the occasion. His sated emotions would have a pleasant little treat. For many a day all pleasures had palled. Now there was something new to live for. He straightened up in the carriage and threw his whole magnetic self into his answers, that self that carried bills through the senate at all odds; that self that had made the conquest of many hearts and ruined many lives. It was not for nothing he had gained his reputation. He knew how to talk. He knew how to make one forget that time was flying. Miriam under cover of the darkness had tried to listen and think at the same time, but in the brilliancy of the Academy she drew her breath and resolutely set herself to listen to all that was said to her. Here she could be seen and she must not let the senator suspect, never, never, never, that she had any trouble. And so she put her whole self into her questions and listened with her eyes as well as with her ears, and more and more as he looked down into those clear, thoughtful eyes and saw the quick play of expression he was pleased that he had come.

There were a few about her whom she knew, and to these she nodded. Her companion bowed and smiled right and left and she knew that she was a center of observation.

She was glad when the first strains of the great orchestra in the opening selection made it possible for her to sit back and keep still. But even then she knew she must keep strict guard over her face. She had often been told that her thoughts were all plainly written there. Claude used to say so. He must not read her heart now. No one must read it. She would lock it away and be false in her face for this night at least. She must think quickly and be ready to act. Senator Bradenberg had said that her husband would meet her at the Academy. When would he come? Would he come alone? He was at Mrs. Sylvester's at dinner. He would likely come with her. She must be expecting that sight and not faint, nor even show the slightest change of expression that it was anything to her. Mrs. Sylvester's box was just opposite. She would be able to see them without lifting her eyes, without showing that she saw them.

And even as she thought it two figures appeared in that box, and she knew without looking that it was her husband and beside him, tall and fair and handsome in a clinging dress of heavenly blue, was Mrs. Sylvester. Her white silk opera cloak was over Claude's arm, and her white glove touched him on the shoulder and pointed something about the arrangement of the chairs where they were to sit. But Miriam was listening with

rapt face to the music—music which she did not hear—
and apparently saw them not. Several eyes were turned
toward her as the smiling beauty and the dark-haired
man with the set face entered the box, and Miriam bore
the scrutiny well. Even the man by her side, watching
her narrowly, could not decide whether she had seen
them yet.

Not until the music had ceased and the applause was
over did she raise her eyes in a studied circuit and let
them travel unconcernedly over the boxes, and rest for
just an instant on the face of her husband as he sat uncomfortably in the background, and then pass on as if
she had taken no note. But her heart was freezing, freezing, and she was glad that she could turn to the senator
and begin to talk or she felt sure she would lose consciousness.

She wondered vaguely what Claude would do if she
should faint and then she forced herself to listen to what
was being said.

CHAPTER 11

•

At Cross Purposes

Oh! we're sunk enough here, God knows! but not
    quite so sunk that moments,
Sure though seldom, are denied us, when the spirit's
    true endowments
Stand out plainly from its false ones, and apprise if
    pursuing
Or the right way or the wrong way, to its triumph or
    undoing.

There are flashes struck from midnights, there are fire-
    flames noondays kindle,
Whereby piled-up honors perish, whereby swollen
    ambitions dwindle;
While just this or that poor impulse, which for once
    had play unstifled,
Seems the sole work of a lifetime that away the rest
    have trifled.

                        —*Robert Browning.*

Claude Winthrop's face was stern and his nerves were
tense as he seated himself on the edge of a chair and
began to search the audience for his wife's face. He
would not even rest his whole weight upon the chair,
but as people do when under excitement he seemed to
think that he could help himself by working with every
muscle of his body. He paid little heed to the beautiful
woman by his side, and saw only to be chagrined by it,
the attention that was called to their box, as this one and
that, even those who were not friends of Mrs. Sylvester
turned and gazed, or bowed across the sea of hands.

He was so confused that he could not distinguish persons. One face melted into another in a dizzy whirl. In vain he searched impatiently for the one face that he desired to see. He could not find it. Once he thought he caught a familiar expression but some one leaned forward and hid it from his sight, and he searched without avail in the same spot for several minutes. His brows drew down in a decided scowl. Mrs. Sylvester began to fear that she would not be able to coax him into being agreeable. She leaned toward him and made some laughing remark but he only scowled the harder and did not reply. He had begun a systematic search of the audience. Mrs. Sylvester had not told him whom she had sent as an escort for his wife. She had laughingly put him aside saying he would see in good time, and he was too angry to ask her again. He tried to recall where his wife had told him their seats were located, but everything of the morning except things that he did not wish to remember, seemed dimmed by the happenings of the day. She would not have chosen expensive seats he felt sure. He began in the humbler seats and went from face to face looking carefully, lest by any chance he should miss her. He dreaded, as he hoped, to find her. What did she think of him? Did she know where he had been detained? What message had Mrs. Sylvester sent? It was likely she had done it up all right, and thrown Miriam entirely off the track, for she seemed to suppose that this was what he wished, and he, fool and weakling that he was, had not had the courage to tell her it was not. It was likely Miriam would not suspect anything, nevertheless he felt that this state of things was not conducive to the confidential relations which he wished to re-establish with his wife. How glad he was that the music kept up. He would not have to talk until he found her. He could not tell from his wife's face whether she was angry or grieved. He hurried his eyes along the next row and morbidly fearing he had missed a few faces went conscientiously back over it again.

"Claude, you positively do look too bearish to endure. You really must moderate that frown," said Mrs. Sylvester leaning toward him again. "If you don't I shall be sorry I brought you."

"I am sorry already," he wished to say, and bit his lips that he had not the courage. He had never known before what a coward he was. After regarding him a moment the lady added:

"If it is on your wife's account you are glaring into the audience in that style you are wasting time. I assure you she looks very happy and is perfectly oblivious of you and me. She seems to be enjoying both the music and her companion hugely. Come, cheer up!"

He followed the direction of her glance and suddenly saw his wife. It was just as she raised her eyes in that sweeping survey and looked him full in the face. There was no recognition in hers—there was placid enjoyment in her expression. This might have restored his equilibrium had he not instantly recognized her companion. That silver head was noticeable in any audience. It seemed to the enraged husband as if it shone with unusual brilliancy to-night, as if to call attention to his shame. With an exclamation half under his breath Claude started from his chair. He felt that he must rush down at once and rescue Miriam from the clutches of that vile man. Hardly knowing what he did he threw Mrs. Sylvester's long white cloak away from him to a distant chair. It had slipped down in front of him from the seat where he had put it in his pre-occupation.

"Claude!" Mrs. Sylvester turned with alarm instantly covered by an amused smile, such as an indulgent nurse might wear over a child's antics. "Claude, every one is watching you! For pity's sake remember where you are! Do sit down here beside me and hand me my programme. See, I have dropped it, and be careful, the music is very soft just now. People will hear you if you move the chairs in such a reckless fashion. Senator Bradenberg won't bite. You can safely trust your wife down there until the programme is over. I did not know you were so impulsive!"

She had talked on softly, bringing him back to a sense of his position, until she saw him seated in the chair on her other side and felt reasonably certain that he would remain there for a little while at least. She had not counted on his being so stirred, and felt chagrined at her lack of power to make him forget his wife. It was unfortunate that she had had no one else by but the "bad senator" to send on this errand. She might have known Claude would be squeamish about having his wife's name associated with his. He was a little notorious, but she had not thought it would matter much. She bit her lip in vexation that she had let him know that she had sent the senator. She might have found a way to let him suppose that it was his wife's own choice to go with him. Stay! Could she not do it yet?

"Your wife has resources of her own," she said in a low voice, amusedly. "I see she has scorned advice and chosen her own escort."

With a quick look at her Claude asked:

"Whom did you send, may I ask?"

"Oh, dear me! Don't put on that tremendous voice," was her laughing response, "no one you could possibly object to in the least, but it seems she prefers the senator. There is no accounting for tastes." He looked sharply at her for a minute. It had never occurred to him to doubt her word before, but now he felt uncertain of her. Was this true? Had Miriam refused to go with the person Mrs. Sylvester had sent and preferred Senator Bradenberg? If so things were a thousand times worse than he supposed. Of course Miriam did not know the man she was favoring. Her pure, true nature would shrink from him, he felt sure, if she knew all. But to have her name linked with his before others was gall and wormwood to her husband. For the time being his own offenses became as nothing to this. Men could do a great many things that would not be forgiven in a woman. Woman's nature was pure and true—here he glanced at the woman by his side and was uncertain—and when she fell, great was the fall!

And all this time the senator had watched every movement of the box above him. He knew a jealous look when he saw it. How interesting! A flirtation with a married woman was twice as spicy if there was some opposition, a little intrigue necessary, and even an effort, just at first, to win her attention from her true liege lord. With a glitter in his eye he settled to his pleasant task, in no wise deterred by the unhappy look of Claude Winthrop above him. Was not that young man in company with another married woman? Why should he object to his wife's receiving attention?

And Miriam, while she kept perfect control of her face, knew every movement of her husband. She saw the change at Mrs. Sylvester's command to the seat nearer to her. She saw the apparent good understanding between them—thought she saw, because imagination was all at work on that side, that Claude avoided her eyes, and that he was all deference to his companion. So blind is love sometimes. So wise is wickedness—temptation.

Miriam became aware that Senator Bradenberg was telling some interesting stories to her. She thought he had kind eyes and a pleasant face. She must not for the world let him suspect that she would rather be anywhere else in the world than by his side at that minute. He was a dear old man who was exerting himself to the utmost to make himself agreeable and he would be pained if he knew how she longed to be at home and bury her face in the pillows and weep in the darkness. The phantom of those restful pillows came between her and the singers whenever she dared raise her eyes to see her husband there beside another woman.

The old plunderer of hearts was meditating whether he would venture to ask her to let him accompany her back home, or whether it would be wisest for his purpose to surrender her to her husband this first time, when she turned to him of her own accord with a coaxing smile on her pretty face such as she used to wear as a child when she wanted something very much, before the days came when she was not so sure of having all her wishes.

"Take me home, please, won't you. I want to hear the end of that story you were telling me. My husband will have to go home with Mrs. Sylvester you know, and anyway I want to hear the rest."

He was quick enough not to show his surprise. He

was delighted and he was puzzled. Was that all acting, that innocent pleading look, or was she really interested? He had always flattered himself on being able to win a woman if he tried, but he had supposed this one harder to reach just at the very first. Or was she possibly piqued by her husband's action? Ah! That must be it. He would have to go slowly for a woman with that pure curve of brow was usually wedded to certain narrow laws of life and it was not easy to persuade her that no possible harm could come from the breaking of them.

He acquiesced with charming grace, and because he knew husbands and the world in general, he joined with her in hastening their steps just a trifle at the close.

And so it happened that they were well down the wide staircase on one side when Claude and Mrs. Sylvester appeared high above them at the top of the opposite stairs. Claude had hurried Mrs. Sylvester beyond all endurance. She felt thoroughly vexed with him, and began to think that this was the end of her intrigue after all. He would rush to his wife and confess all, perhaps, and find out that she had not spoken the truth and then farewell to him. Well! Why not! Why did she care? There were others handsomer, with more wealth and standing—let him go. But a tightening of her heart-strings made her feel that she was not ready for that—not yet. Therefore it was with a certain triumph that she watched Miriam descend below them. She looked up, indeed, and nodded her recognition coolly too, as if she had known they were there all the time and did not mind, and went on talking with bright, animated face that her enemy could but acknowledge was beautiful.

They stood in the full light of the main entrance as Claude again appeared in sight at the foot of the stairs. He was just in time to get a glimpse of his wife's face turned smilingly toward her escort's as she stepped into the shadow of the carriage. A moment more and the senator's white hair made a gleam of light as he entered the carriage, and the door was slammed shut. Claude could hear the rumble of the wheels and the subdued clatter of the horses' hoofs as they moved away.

To think of his wife shut into a carriage with such a

man incensed Claude more than anything had ever had the power to do before. He felt as if he must rush after them down the street, crying Help! Murder! Police! Anything to overtake them and get her away from that man.

But what he did was to control himself. His face was deathly white and his eyes, as Mrs. Sylvester looked into them, were angry eyes.

"How silly of you!" she laughed softly in his ear as they waited for her carriage to be called. "She is perfectly able to take care of herself. Didn't you see how well she worked it to get away from you? You ought to be willing she should have a little pleasure, when you are enjoying yourself. I thought that last movement was well done. She will make quite a success in society if she keeps on as she has begun. I am not sure but I shall take her up myself. You surely are in no position, Claude, to object to a little giddiness on her part," and she tapped him familiarly on his arm with her fan as the carriage drove up.

He gravely helped her into the carriage, then giving the word to the footman, "To Mrs. Sylvester's home," he bowed and said to the lady:

"I will wish you good evening, madam," closed the carriage door, and turned away into the dark street, walking as rapidly as possible.

CHAPTER 12

•

More Complications

What so false as truth is,
   False to thee?
Where the serpent's tooth is,
   Shun the tree—

Where the apple reddens,
   Never pry—
Lest we lose our Edens,
   Eve and I.
          —*Robert Browning.*

Miriam had got rid of the senator gracefully, leaving him
with a glow of satisfaction about his *blasé* old heart, and
locked herself into the guest chamber with her grief.
This room was as far from the other bedrooms as the
house would allow. Here she could not be heard if a sob
escaped her.

The house was still and dark when Claude after his
long, breathless walk reached it. He had been too agi-
tated to trust himself in any kind of public conveyance.
He wanted to be alone and to have the physical exertion
of walking to help him grow calm. Inaction was more
than he could bear. He had had enough of that during
the evening. Before he reached home he had gone over
the miserable matter in every possible phase. He had
excused all his own wrong-doing again and again, only
to see himself the next moment in a more miserable, de-
spicable light than ever. He had blamed Miriam, and excused her. He had raged with both the senator and Mrs.
Sylvester until he was weary of the thought of them,

and still he did not come to any conclusion. He began to
dread to meet his wife as he approached the house, for
he knew that she could use scathing words if she chose,
and his own heart told him she had reason. Still, the fact
that he had left Mrs. Sylvester as he had, just now stood
for a great deal in his favor in the summing up of himself
by himself. He almost felt that it undid the past completely. He had been angry, of course, or he would not
have had the courage to do it. But that he did not recognize now. He thought himself strong and noble to have
dismissed her as he had done. It was the end of any
relations with her, for she would consider that he had
insulted her. He thought he knew Mrs. Sylvester well
enough to be sure that her pride was the strongest thing
about her. He had yet to learn that he did not know how
little he knew about women—some women.

He was almost relieved to find the house dark when
he reached home. Miriam had retired. Would she waken
and speak to him? He struck a match and glanced about
the hall and parlor. Miriam's long wrap, a white glove
and a programme of the evening's concert lay on a chair
near the door, proving that his wife had really reached
home. She was not still out in the darkness with that
awful man. In anguish of soul he went upstairs and
found all dark there save a little light in the bedroom.
Miriam, then, had gone to another room. She was angry
or she did not care for him any longer. Which? The terrible thought that Miriam could possibly ever be weaned
from him suddenly struck him with heavy force. It had
not seemed strange to him that he should amuse himself
with a beautiful and attractive woman for a little while
when Miriam was busy at home with the children and
could not give him all the attention he wanted, but to
have her, whom he had always been wont to consider
his devoted slave, relax in her great clinging devotion to
him was another thing. A wife was meant for a life-long
adoration of her husband. It was an indignity to him that
she should have any desire for pleasure in the company
of others than himself. His indignation waxed at the
thought, as his vanity was hurt by the reflection that he
might not be sufficient for all her earthly needs. He was

not naturally a vain man but he had certainly always supposed that he was Miriam's ideal of all the manly virtues. It was terrible to think that this might be otherwise. For once in his life the very depths of his nature were stirred to their utmost. He did not sleep well. He began to tremble over meeting his wife on the morrow. How could he say what he wished to say about Senator Bradenberg when she had seen him in the company of Mrs. Sylvester? How could he open such a subject? How could he justify himself?

With thoughts like these he tossed the long night through and only fell into an uneasy doze as morning was beginning to dawn. The long delayed home-coming kiss to his wife had not yet been given and it began to seem unlikely that it would come soon. He had even forgotten it in the graver questions that were arising.

Miriam forced herself into a sort of gayety in the morning. The long night watch had been a desperate one for her. She had been trying to find out what to do, but her final conclusion had been to bide her time and go on in the way she had set for herself.

There were letters on the breakfast table. She busied herself with them when Claude came in, and thus they met in a constrained calmness that neither felt.

There were invitations. Miriam read them and passed them over for her husband to see. He frowned as he read them and wondered how they came to be sent to them. This belonged to the new order of things of which he did not wish for more until the trouble between himself and his wife was settled. He was puzzled too, at the kind of people that seemed suddenly to have become aware of their existence. They were people who did not often take up the quiet and obscure. He wondered vaguely if Mrs. Sylvester had a hand in it, or the senator, or who?

Then he tried to frame a sentence of warning to his wife, but words would not come. At last he asked lamely:

"Do you know anything about the man who was with you last evening?"

She looked up with cool dignity.

"Why he is a most delightful old gentleman, and he is a very warm friend of your Mrs. Sylvester, is he not?"

The children came trooping in just then and the maid opened the opposite door and brought in the coffee. Claude's face grew deeply red. There was no more to be said then. Miriam did not seem to notice that anything had happened. He ate the very few mouthfuls of breakfast that he took hurriedly, and left the house.

The day was spent in a round of worry. He dreaded to go home because he had not yet decided how to settle matters with Miriam and yet he confidently expected to bring the matter to some kind of a settlement at once.

But there were guests. Miriam explained in a low tone at the door that he had hurried away so in the morning she had forgotten to mention them, and then she slipped back to the parlor and left him scowling. Was it ever to be like this? Were outsiders to invade his world, even in his own house, forever?

During the days that followed the same state of things prevailed between husband and wife. There was always a cool distance, always some one else present, always some invitation or some guest or some excuse. Claude began to understand that it was of a purpose. Such things could not happen continually without a cause. Miriam was showing him that she wished to stay at a distance. She was pleasant, always attentive to his needs, but not with the loving, caressing touch, nor the joy of service for him in her face. He could see that it was simply a part of her housewifely duties and she performed it gracefully as she had grown to perform all her duties of late.

The little afternoon teas that had begun so bravely the day of his arrival in accordance with the advice received from the magazine letter went on. They grew popular. There was a charming informality and simplicity about them that was not always to be found.

Contrary to Claude's expectation the matter with Mrs. Sylvester was not yet ended. After some weeks' silence he received a note from her at his place of business. It read:

DEAR CLAUDE: I hoped you would have recovered from your fit of childishness before this and come to apologize. But I suppose matters are somewhat complicated and it is not so easy to do. However I forgave you without the asking. You were excited and I know you are sorry for your rudeness.

Please run in this afternoon. I want to see you about something very important. If you don't want your wife to find out everything you had better obey this invitation.

Yours as ever,
SYLVIA.

He tore the note into shreds and then sent his office boy on a fool's errand while he burned it scrap by scrap. He ground his teeth angrily and sat down to think what he should do. He did not wish to go near that woman again. His conscience told him that he ought not to do so. But what was he to do and what did she mean by her hint about his wife's knowing? He wished she did know, he told himself, and then spent the remainder of the afternoon in trying to plan how he could prevent her from knowing. At the end he took his hat and hurried, as he had known from the first he would do, to Mrs. Sylvester's. It was a trifle after five o'clock, the hour named, and he rang the bell hastily. He hoped no one was with her. He would get through with her in short order this time. He had planned just how he would do it. He meant to be sharp and to the point. If she threatened to reveal anything he would tell her to go ahead and do her worst, and then he would go home and have it out with Miriam. He wished he had done that long ago. That was what he ought to have done. It was his miserable hesitancy that had made all the trouble. He would be firm this time as he had been at the carriage door that night.

He had just reached this conclusion for the fiftieth time that afternoon when the door was opened—it was too soon for his ring to have been answered unless the footman was in close attendance on the door as during calling hours—he heard the soft rustle of a woman's garments and his wife stood before him!

One instant they stood there face to face, she deathly white, he crimson to the hair and looking as if he had been caught in the greatest crime the world can know. He could not get his voice nor command his brain. He felt stunned. Before he could come to himself she had forced a smile—such a wan, wild smile—and flitted by him like a spectre.

He turned, coming to himself. A carriage had driven up to the curb. He had noticed it in the street before. Miriam was getting in.

"Miriam!" he called in anguish and ran down the steps at a bound, but she was in and had closed the door with a click, and the driver started up his horse. It was a hired carriage from the livery around the corner from them. Miriam had not looked up nor given any sign that she knew him since that glance in the doorway. It contained reproach and wounded pride and hurt love and sense of deep injury received, all in one. It seemed to him he could never forget that look.

He suddenly became aware that Mrs. Sylvester's footman was standing with respectful curiosity in the door waiting for him to enter, and there he stood looking after that vanishing carriage and knowing not what to do.

For an instant his impulse led him to go in and tell that false woman exactly what he thought of her, and then the sight of the carriage as it turned the corner drove all else from his mind. He must not let Miriam get out of his sight. With a mad idea of overtaking her he started down the street. Afterward it seemed to him he had fled from the house which had stood for temptation to him.

He grew calmer soon and realized that he could never overtake that swift carriage. It had turned and turned again, and he had lost sight of it. To the best of his ideas it did not seem to be on the way home. But he must go there at once. He must be there when Miriam came home if possible. He would meet her and tell her all. There should be no weak delay any more. This must end at once. He was being well punished for all the sins he had ever committed, he told himself.

He had passed through moods enough for a year of time before he reached his home. He felt more weary than he remembered to have felt for years when he applied his latch-key to the door and let himself in.

The light was turned low in parlor and hall as if awaiting the moment when it would be needed, and there was a reassuring whiff of something savory from the regions of the dining room. There was something substantial and sweet in the home atmosphere, all light and warmth, with a chatter of children's voices above like the babbling of a merry little brook, that gave him confidence. Strange he had not noticed before how sweet and safe it all was. Strange he had ever cared for anything else than this that was all his! But *was* it his? The question brought a twinge of fear. Was it possible he was about to lose, nay, had already lost, the center and source of all this—his wife's love?

He settled down in a large arm-chair and rested his head back against the cushiony top. How tired he was! He dropped his eyelids with a sense of relief and wished that he might also drop his burdens as easily. Oh, if Miriam would but come softly up behind as she used to do and kiss his eyelids—so! How sweet, how infinitely sweet, it had been! And he had scorned it for the touch of that other woman's proud lips even for a few days! How impossible it seemed to him now to choose such a course.

He waited a few minutes with his overcoat still on thinking to hear the carriage drive up to the door, for he had been sure when he entered that Miriam was not yet in the house, by a hundred little signs and sounds. He could always tell when his wife was near without needing to see or hear her. The children's voices sounded weary and not glad as when with her. What a mother she had been! Why had he never taken time to be thankful for that? For he loved his children though he had paid very little attention to them lately.

But it occurred to him that he had been out of touch

with Miriam for some time. Perhaps his senses for detecting her presence were not so keen as formerly. She might be in the house and he not know it, after all. He rang the bell to inquire, but when the maid appeared she said Mrs. Winthrop had not yet returned from calling.

He tramped up and down the pretty parlors, his watch in his hand, and looked first from one window and then the other. At last he took his hat and went out again. He could not stand this inaction another minute. A hundred frightful fancies were surging through his brain. He remembered Miriam's intense, impulsive nature in her youthful days. There was no telling but she had been led to do something desperate. Of course that was all fancy, but he must set his mind at rest. He could not have her out in the dark alone with such thoughts of him in her heart as he knew she must have. Down deep in his innermost soul he began for the first time to have some twinges of shame and sorrow for the way he had brought her to this agony, began to despise himself just a little, as he would have despised another man who had done the same thing.

With troubled brows drawn together he paused on the street corner and looked this way and that, trying to stop even the beats of his heart that he might listen if a carriage was coming. But no such welcome sound greeted his ear. Then he formed his plan hastily. He must go back to where he had last seen the carriage and try to trace it. Perhaps she was in need of his help somewhere at that minute.

He walked rapidly now, forgetting his weariness, not thinking to gain time by taking a car or calling a cab. It seemed to him he was more likely to accomplish something on his feet. It was a relief to his tense, strained nerves to be on the move.

When he arrived at the corner near the Sylvester mansion all was still and dark, with twinkling lights glimmering down among the shadowed streets. There was nothing to show where the carriage had passed a little over two hours before. Of course there was not. He might have known that. Why had he come here—of all places? He was losing his head.

He looked toward the wide windows of the beautiful house in the next block where the soft roseshaded lights proclaimed a life of ease, and as he turned his head quickly away he breathed in his heart a great curse on the woman who had wrought this mischief, and immediately after upon himself for having been so weak as to have been led by her.

Back he took his weary way once more, following every turn which the carriage might have taken, as a dog follows a lost scent, and always back to the main way home again. And behind him followed on his trail those horrid wolves of fears and fancies—the thought of what might have happened to Miriam.

CHAPTER 13

·

In the Serpent's Toils

Poor little heart!
  Did they forget thee?
Then dinna care! Then dinna care!
Proud little heart!
  Did they forsake thee?
Be debonair! Be debonair!
          —*Emily Dickinson.*

When Miriam gave the hasty order to the driver to go to her aunt's house on the west side of the city she had it in mind merely to make time to think before there would be any possible chance of seeing her husband or children or even her servants again. It was a long drive to Cresson Avenue, and her mind might become clearer by the time she reached there and she be able to mark out some course for herself. At the moment she was conscious of but one thing, and that was that the worst had happened. Her fears, which she now knew to have been but fears and not certainties, were confirmed at last, and in such a way that there was no more room left for hope. She knew that in all the weary work of her carefully planned campaign she had been upheld by one great, strong hope, and that was that her husband was true to her after all and that in some mysterious way the trouble would be all explained so that there would finally come a glad morning after her night of sorrow. Now hope was stricken, never to rise again, she felt sure. Could the enemy have been permitted then to look into Miriam Winthrop's heart she would have exclaimed in joyful triumph that her victory was complete.

Miriam sank back in the carriage, having first drawn the curtains, hid her face in her hands and shuddered—shuddered until she felt she was going into a nervous chill. Then suddenly she remembered that there was a great affair on hand that evening—one of the first of the really great functions to which she and Claude had been invited since her venture into the world. It was to be an affair of hundreds, not of tens, and its greatness consisted in the home in which it was held and in the very select company who were invited. It meant much to the success of her schemes that she had been invited thére. She had not dared to hope for an invitation, and had wondered ever since it came to whom she owed the honor.

This gathering, which a few hours before had meant so much to her, had suddenly become as nothing. But somehow the memory of it recalled her to the exact situation and enabled her to gain command of herself and look things in the face.

Gradually the whole thing became clear to her. She must hold down her feelings till she was sure what she ought to do and not act rashly. In the meantime, it would not do to let her enemy see her defeat. She must wear a brave front and not give up the battle even though she felt that all was lost. Better to die fighting than that. The party, at least, must be gone through with, till she could get time to think. Mrs. Sylvester, who would be sure to be there—and a sudden thought like a dart made her sure to whom she owed the invitation—should see her smiling and unabashed, even though Mrs. Sylvester might have looked from her richly curtained windows but a few minutes before and seen the last prop swept from her hope.

But how could she go with Claude after what had happened? Of course she had ridden many times in a carriage with him during the last few weeks in a silence that was painful to both, or in constrained conversation of which neither took much account. She had been able to keep him at a distance when nothing had passed between them to give tangible expression to the chasm that lay between their love. But now, after what had happened, she felt she could not ride with him that night. It would be impossible for her to control herself. Besides, she doubted if he would come home at all, much less accompany her to the party. Some other way must be thought out. Could she take the maid? But no, she was not trained, and the nurse was away with her sick mother. The children must not suffer, whatever happened.

Could she inveigle her aunt into going with her? No; for her aunt would ask a hundred troublesome questions, and she was noted for sharp eyes and a sharper tongue. She would pry something out of her niece before she granted any favors. Her aunt would not do.

She pushed up the silken curtains of the carriage and looked into the street. She was surprised to find how dark it had grown. They were driving more slowly now over a rough pavement by tall houses. It was some minutes before Miriam could make out the locality.

Then a great club-house loomed up, brilliant with its many windows and its lavish display of electric lights. In the arched marble entrance night was made into day. A profusion of flowers and palms veiled some of the windows, and the liveried servants moving here and there, at the doorways or in the distance behind the windows, gave some hint of what man's idea of a heaven upon earth might be.

Miriam's notions of a club-house were vague and a little fearful, but it was a part of the world into which she had entered, and she looked curiously, and wondered if Claude had found his way in there, and if this grandeur had made him dissatisfied with all that his home could give. Her sad eyes looked intently at the windows, noted the elegance and ease that seemed to pervade even the entrance-way to the place, and her heart sank. How little and how ignorant had she been to think to go against a world such as this was. Even for her one precious love she had been worse than foolish to try against such odds.

Then, just as they were passing the last window she saw a gleam of white hair, and a familiar face below coming down the marble steps.

A quick resolve came to her aid. Here was help. She would make an appeal to Senator Bradenberg.

She stopped the driver and explained to him that she wished to speak to the gentleman just coming down the steps, and the gallant senator was by her side in an instant, his hat lifted in deference.

In the brilliant light that came from the arch over the entrance Miriam's face shone distinctly. There was not a trace in the lustrous eyes of the storm through which she had been passing, save a feverish light that but made them brighter. The excitement of the moment had brought out the clear red of the cheeks, and the senator voted her for the hundredth time a very beautiful woman.

There was a childlike innocence in her appeal that saved her from any hint of suspicion of motives not the highest.

"Are you going to the Washburns' to-night, and have you promised to escort any one? Because if you haven't won't you please take me? Circumstances have arranged themselves in such a way that it will be impossible for my husband to accompany me. I shall be ready to start by nine o'clock. Now tell me frankly, please, if you have another engagement, or I shall never ask you again. You have been so good a friend, you know, that I have made bold to appeal to you, as I happened to see you in passing. You see I began to fear I might not get there at all."

The senator beamed. If he had other engagements he chose to keep them in the background. He was a man whose engagements were always subject to his own pleasure in the matter. He felt that Miriam's appeal gave him a decided advantage over this beautiful woman, and his eyes gleamed with a light that was not wholly saintly as he responded graciously that he would be charmed to accompany her to the Washburns'. He blessed the happy circumstances that had made him her choice.

He studied her face keenly with his hawk eyes to see if there was aught between herself and her husband that could give him more advantage with her, and he pressed her hand with a lingering tenderness wholly unnecessary as he paid her a pretty compliment. Then the carriage moved on, and Miriam was wrapped in the darkness of her thoughts once more, giving no heed to the lover-like words that had been murmured in her ear by the "dear kind old man," as she phrased it to herself.

Miriam reviewed with burning brain and nerves held in control like a vise, the movements it would be necessary for her to make. The gown she was to wear lay at this moment in her dressing room, the crowning creation of her skillful fingers. On it had been put more expense than all her other wardrobe together, and into it was woven the most careful and laborious needlework of which she was capable. In her own mind, after the experience she had had so far, it compared well with the costly imported robes the rich ones wore. It was filmy and encrusted here and there, not too much, with the frost-like lace-work carefully chosen and curiously blended with the lace-work of the owner's own daring fingers. It was white, all creamy white, and out of it her well-set shapely head had risen like a queen's when last she tried it on. Her dark, rich hair would set all off. She was almost sure the garment would be a success. But a daring thought for her was hovering in her breast. It was to bare her neck and arms. She had not done it before, for all the prejudices of her up-bringing in a country town where tradition did not call such dress modest, had been against it, and though she had deferred to inexorable custom by having her evening dresses made low, she had invariably managed to fill the vacant space with something soft and white which, while a cover, was yet a concession. And for her arms, gloves and lace made it quite possible to keep one's ideals even in a world where such notions were at a discount.

But now her eyes gleamed in the darkness. It seemed to her a devil perhaps might be whispering the suggestion. A daring like none she had ever felt before came to her. She would do it. Claude should see her in the same way in which he saw Mrs. Sylvester. He should see that his wife's neck was as white and her arms as well rounded as those of her adversary. For once she would appear as did others. If she was to die fighting, and she felt it was near the end of the battle now, whatever the result, she would die brilliantly. Any scruples she might have had before had fled. What were scruples at such a time? If it was this that Claude admired he should see that his wife could be as beautiful as any. She would die leaving him with the pain of regret in his heart.

The turning of the carriage from the smooth asphalt pavement to the cobblestones reminded her suddenly that she was nearing her aunt's, and that now she had no desire to see that excellent woman. She leaned forward and by the light of the passing street lamps examined her watch. It was growing late. She must hurry home to dress or she would not be ready when the senator came.

She gave the direction to the coachman, who occupied his homeward ride in some very uncomplimentary reflections on "parties who never knew their own minds," and settled herself to relax perfectly and rest during the homeward ride.

It was an evidence of the wonderful control she had acquired over herself during the last few months that she was able to do this in the face of all she had gone through and all that was yet to come.

Arrived at home she went at once to her room, and the first thing she did after locking her door and turning up the gas, was to cut with determined hands the carefully arranged white drapery from the neck and sleeves of her dress. She held her breath as she did it lest her courage fail, and she crushed the soft mass into a hopeless heap in the waste-basket lest she should be tempted to replace it. Then with bated breath she set about her preparations.

There was no thought of the untasted dinner. She did not remember it till the maid, coming at her summons to help fasten her gown, spoke of it. Then she answered that she was detained elsewhere and could not get home for dinner. She did not question if her husband had returned. It did not occur to her that he might have done so. She felt almost certain he had stayed with Mrs. Sylvester. She had not permitted herself one backward glance from her fast-moving carriage that afternoon.

The discreet maid said nothing. She saw that her mistress was at high pressure. She noticed with satisfaction that the shrouding white had been removed from the neck of the dress. She was glad that at last the world would have a chance to see that Mrs. Winthrop was a handsome woman, and knew how to dress as well as any one.

The toilet was interrupted only by the arrival of a box of most exquisite white orchids with Senator Bradenberg's card. With the light of battle still in her eyes, Miriam fastened them in place as one more weapon wherewith to dazzle the enemy, and as she did so blessed the "kind old man" for having selected these costly flowers, which otherwise she could never have hoped to wear.

It was the one touch the costume needed. Miriam stood a moment and gazed startled at her own beauty. She scarcely knew herself. She seemed to be looking at some other person critically, and to be more than satisfied. The color in her cheeks from intense excitement was more beautiful than any artist could have painted it, the lustre of her eyes beyond the power of any drug to produce.

"You should let the children see you, ma'am, before you go," said the maid in admiration. "Miss Pearl is likely to be awake yet, and Celie would soon hush off to sleep again."

But Miriam shuddered. Let her little innocent children look upon her so? Never! The white neck and arms that gleamed at her from the glass seemed dreadful to her when she realized that she was throwing in what conscience she had left. She had staked all, and it must be win or lose to-night. This she said to her heart as she looked steadily into her own eyes in the glass.

She turned away and let the maid wrap about her shoulders the long, white cloak, and said:

"No, don't waken the children. I would rather they would sleep. You need not sit up for me, I may be late. Be sure the baby is well covered."

Then she went down to meet her escort who had arrived and take her seat in the carriage, and the door was slammed shut and she whirled away in the darkness.

Five minutes afterward Claude once more reached his own door, weary and faint and frightened.

CHAPTER 14

·

The Washburn Party

Hold me but safe again within the bond
Of one immortal look! All woe that was,
Forgotten, and all terror that may be,
Defied—no past is mine, no future: look at me!

· · · · · · ·

When I saw him tangled in her toils,
A shame, said I, if she adds just him
To her nine and ninety other spoils,
The hundredth for a whim!

—*Robert Browning.*

Claude Winthrop's sharpened ears had caught the sound of carriage wheels as he neared his own street. It was a welcome sound, and he began to berate his wife in his heart for giving him such an evening of suspense, and, in spite of his own repentings, he forgot at once that he was the cause of the trouble and put it upon her.

He heard the carriage door shut and the rumble coming toward him, and looked keenly at the driver as the dark object came in sight. Was it the same carriage in which Miriam had gone out that afternoon, and where had she been all this time? Then just in front of a street lamp the carriage passed him and he caught the gleam of white hair and a graceful head bent in deference as only the bad senator could do, and caught a gleam of something white beyond him, and a face out of the darkness, and then sudden fear took hold upon him.

He hastened his steps with renewed vigor, and fairly shook the door open when his fumbling key refused to give him entrance at once.

"Where is Mrs. Winthrop?" he demanded of the startled maid as she appeared in answer to his ring.

"Why sir, she's gone. She told me you were detained, and the carriage has come and she's gone."

"Gone?" he echoed the words wildly, his blood-shot eyes and haggard face making the girl wonder if he had been drinking.

"Why, gone to the Washburn party, of course," she answered, edging nearer to the dining-room door.

Claude Winthrop tore off his overcoat and went upstairs two steps at a time. He rushed from room to room as if he hoped to find her there. Gradually it was dawning upon him that they had been going to the Washburns' this night. He had forgotten until now. But Miriam had not. It seemed she had gone despite what had happened that afternoon. It came to him bitterly that she was able to face society with what there was between them. It showed him plainly, he thought, that she had long understood all that his call that afternoon upon Mrs. Sylvester had meant to her. In sudden sharp fear the possibility that she did not care so much as he had supposed she would was presented to his mind.

The light was still burning brightly in her dressing-room, and on the dressing table lay the pasteboard box from which she had taken the orchids. One poor flower had been slightly bruised, and she had left it lying with the senator's card, carelessly, on the tissue paper of the box. Claude caught up the card and read, and horror choked him, and a fire flamed up into his eyes. If Senator Bradenberg had been present just then it might not have been well with him.

Half frenzied the husband tore through the rooms again, in the vain search for something to prove that it was not true, that she was yet there, and he might explain and all be made right between them, for he seemed to know that he would never be at rest again until that peace had come. It was a sign of the stirring of good in his heart that he now began to have a little doubt as to whether this might ever be.

He went to the nursery at last. He touched the cool foreheads of his boy and girl as they lay in their first sound sleep, and then bent over the crib where lay his baby. And it was in her soft neck, with her gold curls folding all about his hot, tired eyes, and her sweet breath coming and going regularly like the breath from a meadow at evening when the cows are coming home, that he was first able to think, and that a kind of repentance for what had happened began to stir him to better things.

It was not long he stayed there, but he gained strength to think, and then knew that he must get him to the Washburn house with all possible speed. The gay throng was the last place he would have chosen in his present state of mind, but he felt it imperative that he see his wife at once and bring her home. After that all should be made straight before he slept.

He kissed little Celia tenderly and went swiftly to make his own toilet.

It was not the careful, prolonged affair that Claude Winthrop's toilets were usually, even for an everyday function, and yet this was one of the great crushes of the season. But he did not care now. He was going in search of his wife. A certain amount of care must be taken to gain him entrance and prevent comment, but what mattered the set of his necktie now?

Nevertheless he was delayed by little things, his hands were nervous and trembling with excitement. In his haste he had to undo and do things over again, and he began to feel the lack of his dinner, yet he would not stop to get anything.

And at last he was out on the street and started toward the Washburns'. Even then it seemed to him as if he were treading over and over the same ground like a horse set to saw wood, and did not get on in spite of all his efforts. And when he came in sight of the great house with its canvas-guarded entrance and its many twinkling windows it seemed to him the glitter of a hateful, treacherous trap that had snared his beautiful wife.

The music and the dancing and the pomp and ceremony and feasting were in full sway when he at last entered and began his search.

Then, after all, it was not his wife but Mrs. Sylvester who first met his searching gaze.

She was all in black to-night, black velvet, rich and sweeping and simple, and out of it her white shoulders rose in all their loveliness. The only jewels she wore were a string of diamonds about her throat, and diamonds in the aigrette in her hair. The effect was startling. Claude had never seen her all in black before, for she affected much the dainty shades of blue and pink or white and gold. But it seemed to-night as if she had chosen her costume with a view to dazzling all who beheld her.

In her hand she carried—and Claude could not help but notice—a great handful of delicate lilies of the valley, the flowers he had given Miriam on their wedding day. And alas, the flowers he had often given this other woman too.

It angered him that he noticed her at all, that he saw how beautiful she was, that he did not hate the white hands that held the lilies, the scornful lips that smiled at him, and the treacherous eyes that summoned him so imperatively. It amazed him that in his present state of feeling he could notice details like flowers and recall clearly all the sweetness and the bitter connected with them.

He did not answer her summons. He did not respond to her unspoken greeting across the roomful of unnoticing people. He only drew his brows together in a heavy frown—the frown that some people had remarked upon as being "interesting"—and glowered back, and then turned his restless eyes to search the great ball room once more.

He did not look her way again. He would not, though he was long conscious of her amused gaze still fixed upon him as she talked to a circle of admiring men. It occurred to him that with that same amused smile would she greet death and destruction if they should chance to come her way.

As soon as he could, for the crush, he made his way slowly around the room, but not toward Mrs. Sylvester. Always he kept it in mind to avoid the place where he

had seen her, to avoid it even with his eyes. And thus
moving suddenly she spoke to him, startling him, as
one will start at finding the evil so carefully avoided in
front standing just behind one.

How she had come there he did not stop to question.
He turned upon her angrily.

"Claude, you are a perfect bear! I have come to warn
you to take that frown from your face or you will presently be the subject of comment. What is the matter?
That little meeting with your wife on my doorstep seems
not to have agreed with your fine temper, my dear. Was
she so very angry?"

There was pity in the well-modulated tone, the allur-
ing pity that Mrs. Sylvester knew so well how to use
upon occasion, and it roused the soul of the half-
frenzied man nearly to distraction. He could have struck
her as she stood there in all her insolent beauty, speaking of his peerless wife with such disdain. He could
have struck her, yet the hand that strikes was fettered by
the tender pressures he had once given to her hand, by
the waxen blossoms he had disloyally brought to another than his wife; and the white lips that would have
uttered withering words to her were sealed by the kiss
he had once placed upon her lips. Oh, horror of agony!
How that kiss burned into his lips now and to his very
soul, like the sting of a venomous serpent!

There she stood before him with all her power about
her, all her beauty, all her unscrupulousness, and dared
to be what she was and to look him in the eyes and bid
him follow her.

He turned from her as one would have turned from
some hideous, loathsome sight, and would have moved
away without a word but that she laid her hand upon his
arm and walked beside him, and he could not rid himself of her except by shaking her off and bringing the
eyes of the assembled multitude upon them both. He
was forced to walk beside her, but he did it with his angry eyes fixed straight ahead, and so soon as they were
come to an alcove where it was possible he stepped out
of the crowd and led her to a vacant seat.

She saw that for some strange reason he was proof

against her wiles to-night. He meant to leave her here alone. He had not yielded to her startling beauty. She knew it was startling, she had studied for days to make it so. And yet it had failed!

Failed? Should she entertain such a thought? Not for an instant! Summoning all her arts she said with a piteous little sigh:

"Claude, you must bring me something from the supper room. The heat has made me dizzy and faint. To tell the truth I have been ill for a week, and I only made the effort to get up and come here that I might see you about something very important, and you declined to come and see me, even though I warned you—"

"What shall I bring you?" he cut her short with his icy words as if impatient to have the disagreeable duty done.

"Claude," she said reproachfully, her voice trembling, "you are acting abominably. But I forgive you. Get me something quick, at least a glass of water—" and she leaned back against the cushions and dropped the delicate eyelids for an instant with a flutter of weakness, though her color was too bright for one about to faint.

He cast one glance into her face and thought he detected deceit in her very attitude. But he went at once. Strange he could see so plainly now what but a few short weeks ago had been so charmingly veiled.

He scarcely knew what he got from the supper room, anything to have the hateful duty done and be free, but when he brought it to her Mrs. Sylvester smiled faintly and asked him to sit down beside her for just a minute until she felt better. She took the glass he brought her and sipped a few swallows.

"Wait!" she commanded impressively, suddenly dropping all her smiling ways and taking a new tone with him, "I have something most important to tell you. It will take but a moment, and indeed I must tell you though you do not deserve it."

He waited beside her impatiently. He could do no less after her request although he felt that she was deceiving him merely to keep him there. His natural politeness seemed to make it necessary that he remain for a few

minutes at least, and his cowardly spirit saw no way to
leave. But as she talked his eyes searched the brilliant
moving throng. He scarcely heard what Mrs. Sylvester
was saying, till he became conscious that she was speaking of Miriam:

"Have you seen her yet? She is magnificent. That
gown of hers must have been a fabulous price. It is perfect. Only the greatest artist could have turned it out.
And right there lies her trouble. She is so constantly
with Senator Bradenberg—"

Claude's icy voice broke in upon her voluble talk:

"You will be kind enough to leave my wife's name out
of the conversation."

She had never heard him speak like that. She looked
up at him half-frightened and was not reassured by the
angry eyes that met hers. Her scheme was in danger of
failure, and there was nothing in the world that she
hated worse than failure; besides she had found this flirtation so altogether interesting and so hard to pursue
that her heart—as much of a heart as she possessed—
was affected by it, and when a heart is involved, and
there is no conscience behind it, there is nothing a
woman will not do. She dashed in boldly:

"But I must speak of your wife. Don't you see she will
bring a scandal upon you? You surely are not blind. I feel
it my duty to warn you. I did not dream her innocent
baby-face covered so wise and old a head. It has not
taken her long to learn the ways of the world. She has
cast aside the last vestige of her country prudery to-
night, and her gown is irreproachable—"

At that moment there was a stir among the throng
near them, and the music burst forth loudly. Instinctively Claude leaned forward to catch her words, though
they were making his soul rage within him. Encouraged
by this Mrs. Sylvester went on:

"She has made a wonderful success with nothing to
start on, but she should be warned to go a little slower.
There are other men with whom she might amuse herself, but she is all taken up with the senator and does not
understand. She ought to know that when Senator Bradenberg plays, he plays to kill!"

Trembling with rage, white with horror and fury, Claude essayed to stop her and bent low to speak the words. He felt so angry he would have liked to throttle the white neck in its setting of diamonds.

"Take care what you are saying of my wife, Mrs. Sylvester!" He said the words so quietly that she scarcely realized how intensely he was feeling until she looked into his face and he met her eyes steadily.

What it was just then that made them both look up at the people passing near them neither knew. There was nothing in their coming to attract attention, more than in those that had passed before, but Claude found himself face to face with his wife coming calmly toward him on the arm of the senator, the senator's orchids on her breast, and the senator's glances for her face.

For a moment he looked without knowing what he saw. It seemed to him that she had died and this was her white angel come to reproach him. The filmy robe which he knew not, seemed some angel garment. The bare neck and arms to which he was so unaccustomed, all made her seem unreal. He gazed and gazed as she came nearer, lost in admiration of her beauty, until she was near enough to touch him, and then she looked up unconsciously, took in coolly the situation, nodded to Mrs. Sylvester, passed by her husband's searching gaze as though he had been a stranger, and with slightly heightened color, her small white hand resting confidently upon the soft broadcloth of the senator's arm, passed on into the conservatory.

CHAPTER 15

•

Villainy Foiled

I took my power in my hand
And went against the world;
'Twas not so much as David
   had,
But I was twice as bold.

I aimed my pebble, but myself
Was all the one that fell.
Was it Goliath was too large,
Or only I too small?
                    —*Emily Dickinson.*

When Miriam had felt herself shut into the carriage on
the way to the Washburns' two hours before, she leaned
back against the cushions and closed her eyes in a mo-
mentary relief. She had been under so intense a strain
for so many hours that she was glad of the minute's relief from glaring light and necessity for action.

It was before she had opened her eyes that the senator
bent over her with his tender: "You are very weary, poor
child!" and the carriage passed Claude in the uncertain
lamplight.

She roused herself to be an interested listener to her
companion, wishing all the time it had been possible for
her to take this ride without an escort. What a relief it
would have been to just shut her eyes and rest without
even trying to think, all the way. For she felt instinctively
that the evening was to be an ordeal.

"I *am* tired," she said smiling and trying to rally her
forces to seem gay. "I have been having a full day."

"Well, lean back and rest. You need not mind me. Don't feel that you must keep up now to hide your feelings. I know through what a strain you are passing. You are a brave woman."

Horror froze Miriam's veins. Her heart almost stopped beating for the moment. A numbness crept up from her finger tips tingling through her whole being. She started upright in her seat and her face grew white in the dim darkness of the carriage so that her companion wondered if perhaps he might have gone too far.

He knew? He had seen her trouble? Then the whole world must know. Then her secret was out, and her defeat was an accomplished thing already, without the evening's test. Claude was fallen and her heart was desolate! And yet she found that she had still been clinging to that poor dead hope that she had declared gone forever so many, many times.

For the instant she longed to return home and hide her heart where no eye might look upon her defeat, no scornful lips speak to others of her shame. Then the steady control into which she had been schooling herself for weeks took command and she rallied. Not for the world would she give sign that she recognized her defeat. She would go through this one evening with her head held as bravely as though her heart were crowned with happiness. She would not give a sign or quiver, though the knife went twisting through her heart again and again. So would she at least make glorious her defeat.

"Oh, 'tis not so bad as that!" she laughed gayly, and wondered at herself that her voice could assume so much; "but I have been accepting too many invitations perhaps, and the sudden change from my quiet life with my children during the last few years has been a little hard."

The worldly wisdom that covered all the meaning of her companion's pity had not been acquired for nothing. It was better after all that she should spend her time in mental fencing with the senator than that she should have time to rest and think, as think she must, however much she might wish to cease.

Senator Bradenberg admired her bravery, wondered if it were wholly brave or wholly innocent, and pleased himself all the more with the prospect of the conquest of this charming woman in the near future.

He had but to play his cards well, and she would be won—all the more interesting that she was not easy to conquer. Once she found out that her husband was on intimate terms with a woman like Mrs. Sylvester she would turn to him for comfort. Then he would have it all his own way. In his long career there had been few that he had cared to smile upon who had been able to resist him.

He saw that she did not intend to give him her confidence at present, and gracefully led the conversation from the dangerous point, yet always keeping in it that tender personal note, whose main impression was that he was ready to do anything in her service.

He told her how it had touched his heart that she had chosen him to take her out to-night, that he had felt from the first moment of meeting her that there was something drawing them toward one another, she reminded him so strikingly of a dear lost sister. Oh, that dear lost sister who had never existed except in his fertile brain, and oh, the long list of beautiful women who were like her! He told her how he had been watching her, and how beautiful she was, and what a success in society, and how pleased he was that she had chosen to wear his poor flowers on her heart—"as a shield, my dear, use them as a shield, if you please, against anything that might trouble you," and then, as she murmured her thanks for words she had only half heard because her mind was traveling on ahead of the carriage and she was planning the last scene of the conflict, he took her little hand and pressed it gently and stroked it with his well-tended fingers and told her she was to turn to him when anything arose to give her any trouble, that he could always be relied upon. And could he have known that Miriam was thinking much more about how she could get her hand away without hurting the kind old man's feelings than she was of his words, he would not have smiled so confidently as he handed her from the carriage, nor would his sensual eyes have looked at her with half the light of triumph that they held.

He was kindness itself during the evening. He did not keep her entirely to himself for it was not his way to call too much attention when he was in the way of a conquest. There were people who delighted to warn young innocents against bad wolves. He had no desire to have anything interfere with his plans. Therefore he kept them to himself, and played the quiet, elderly escort to perfection. He so managed that Mrs. Winthrop was always the center of a group of people worth knowing; he seemed to be not too much in evidence, and yet he was on hand at the right moment to serve her. He sent her down to supper with another man on purpose, and watched her from afar with gloating eyes. When she had appeared from the dressing room and he saw that she had modified her way of dress to suit the most exacting laws of society his heart had leaped in something like the way it did in youthful days. She was learning fast. One more barrier was broken down. How lovely she was, and what incomparable arms and what finely modeled shoulders. Could Claude have seen his evil gaze just then he would certainly have knocked him down.

All the evening the senator watched for his moment, not sure yet that it would come to-night or even in many nights—watched until he saw the weary look coming more and more into the beautiful dark eyes; watched until the pitiful, white quiver became more distinct about the firm, sweet mouth; watched until he saw Claude enter, and saw Mrs. Sylvester's maneuvers, and until those two went to the alcove by the conservatory entrance. Then he felt that his time had come.

Slowly and with careful calculation he made his way to Miriam's side and murmured low to her that there were some beautiful orchids, rarer even than those she wore, in the conservatory, and as she looked tired would she like to come and see them? And she assented eagerly. She had caught glimpses of Mrs. Sylvester on one side of the room and her husband on the other a few minutes before, and every instant since had been of agonizing expectation. The crisis, she felt, was just at hand.

Almost she felt her heart fail her. She fain would get a minute away from all this glare and noise before it came. And then they passed the alcove and she saw her husband apparently in deep conversation with her enemy.

The senator, watching her closely, saw the magnificent way in which she passed the ordeal, and then saw the white stealing about her mouth in deathly, haggard lines. Almost he thought she would fall and he led her to a seat behind some palms in a turn of the walk, out of the way of most of the guests.

It was a true lover's retreat where he had placed her, in a chair of many soft cushions, and he took the delicate fan from her hand and wafted it gently till she seemed to gain a little courage to look up, a piteous appeal in her eyes.

He did not quite understand that appeal. He took it as a signal for his own plans to begin.

"My dear," he said placing an arm on the back of her chair and letting his fingers touch the white shoulder near them, "don't look so pitiful. There are other loves in this world, even if one has failed. I told you you might turn to me and I have felt from the first that you would do so. My dear, I love you as he, whose name you bear, could never do. Will you come with me and let me comfort you?" and then he leaned over her and pressed a kiss upon her horrified lips.

If all the terror of all the women in this world who have been sinned against could have been concentrated in one look, that look was Miriam Winthrop's. Consternation, dismay, loathing, and alarm were mingled in one mighty, fascinated gaze. It was the look of one who, having fled from pursuing terror, encounters a beast of prey more fearful than anything that could have gone before.

Miriam had shuddered as his evil fingers touched her cold shoulder. It was a liberty which even an old man should not have taken, she thought; and then as the meaning of his words became clear at last to her she watched him with horrified, wild gaze, seeming to see the very glare of the lower regions in his wicked eyes. Noticing as one will the details of insignificant things at such a time, she saw a miniature, reflected in the crystal discs of his eyeglasses, the ballroom beyond, with its gayly moving throngs, the dancers, the flutter of fans, the turning of heads, the slow walk of couples near the entrance of the conservatory, the sharp-pointed palms towering all about, and two tall figures in black coming toward them. All the time she saw these things she felt that the minute for this human tiger to spring was coming, and her life would depend upon whether she was able to evade his horrid clutch.

She was utterly unprepared for the kiss, but her senses were on the alert. All these months of agony and silent self-control had been, as it were, schooling her to meet this awful minute. All the sorrow she had suffered as she came up, step by step, this long dark way of trouble had been as nothing to the torture of the present development. Just where she had trusted the most had she found treachery the basest.

One instant she crouched in the chair after that shameful touch of his lips and then, darting upward with all the litheness of her girlhood days, she raised her firm hand and struck the elegant and ardent senator in the face; struck him full in the eyes where the two fragile discs balanced on their slender nose-piece of gold across his aristocratic nose, and sent the glasses shivering in a myriad pieces on the marble floor, and a trickle of blood down the senator's baffled, astonished face showed that the glass had done its work before it reached the floor.

Then Miriam turned and, panting, wildly fled.

The senator, wiping his blinded eyes and stinging cheeks in bewilderment, looked up to see two people standing at the entrance to their retreat. And one was fair and tall and clad in black velvet and wore a devilish smile of amusement on her face, but the other had angry eyes that blazed from a face as white as death.

The senator was searching vainly in his fertile brain for an explanation that should allow him to assume his usual careless ease. It is safe to say he had not been many times slapped in the face for a kiss. He would have given much to know how long these spectators had been present.

But Miriam, flying down between the palms, all white—white face, white arms, white gown, the light of holy anger springing from her sorrowful eyes, like some desecrated angel, tearing, as she flew, the hateful blossoms from her breast and stamping on them, looked up and saw her husband standing before her, and beside him saw her enemy and knew her hour had come and her defeat complete, with all the witnesses present. As though she had been struck to the heart, she dropped silently at his feet, striking her head heavily on the marble floor.

Darting one awful look of imprecation and revenge, Claude stooped and gathered her in his arms and felt the unresponsive heart.

And behind him stood that silent figure in black velvet, with the same scornful smile upon her lips, the only witness of the first flush of humiliation on the face of the usually complaisant senator, and the first white agony of the terrified husband.

This was her work, and she viewed it with the cruel scorn of a heartless woman.

CHAPTER 16

•

Fighting Death

The small neglect that may have pained,
A giant structure will have gained
When it can never be explained.
                        —*A. D. F. Randolph.*

They were all sympathy in a moment, the crowd outside
that surged about to help, but some glanced curiously at
Mrs. Sylvester and then at Claude, and others looked
beyond to where the senator searched for the frame of
his eye-glasses, the while he concocted a fine tale of how
they were broken as he tried to save Mrs. Winthrop from
falling, and told it too, to those who came to help him
look. For he was shut in from escape at present unless
he crawled behind the palms, which he would have
been glad to do.

A doctor was found somewhere in the hushed throng,
who cleared a space for air and gave opportunity for the
abashed old scoundrel to slip away.

But Mrs. Sylvester did not move. Claude once, on
looking up, while the doctor was listening to the heart to
see if there was any movement at all, saw her standing
there and hated her. He wished she would go and leave
him alone with his misery and his dead life, she who
had brought him here to meet his just punishment and
who had stayed to see it meted out to him stroke by
stroke.

Some one gave an order for a carriage and Celia
Lyman brought the soft white cloak that Miriam had in-
geniously made to imitate a much costlier one, and Mrs.

121

Sylvester still stood and watched, not offering to be of any assistance, only smiling that perpetual amusement which almost seemed as if her eyes were glad of all this mischief.

They carried Miriam to the carriage by a side entrance and the doctor went with them to take her home.

And as long as she could see them down the long palm arch of the conservatory, Mrs. Sylvester watched them. Then she turned and went back to the ballroom, but her hands were empty. She had lost somewhere her lilies of the valley.

Back through the darkness of the streets rode Miriam, resting at last from all the weary way and in her husband's arms; back from her glorious defeat, where she had come out from the world's smirching as white in soul as were her garments.

The doctor kept his practised finger upon the place where the pulse should have been, but only a feeble, occasional flutter gave any hope that there was life. The long day's strain, with the tremendous happenings, added to the months of agony, had secured the inevitable result. The poor weak body and tortured soul had given way and were almost at the parting place.

They carried her in and up the staircase down which she had come so beautiful and so sorrowful but a few short hours before, and the household was awakened to that hushed excitement that pervades the home where death is lingering on the threshold.

The frightened servants obeyed orders, went on errands, brought stimulants and blankets and hot water.

All night they worked, the doctor and a nurse and another doctor, who had been summoned to their aid. The husband stood helpless at the foot of the bed and watched his wife's white face that seemed to be modeled in marble, so still it was and unearthly in its spotless reproach. And was this the end then? Was he no more to see her on earth? Never to have a chance to explain—no, there was no explanation—but to tell her that he loved her? Was not this punishment too great for all he had done, for his weakness, his cowardice? Nay, but what had he made her suffer! spoke the white face on the pillow to his shrinking heart.

And little Pearl stole from her bed in her long nightdress and crept her soft little hand in his and whispered:

"Is our mamma dead, father? Why doesn't she wake up?"

And even the sorrowing, gentle little voice seemed to accuse him of the deed.

The long hours dragged away and still there was no sign from her that she lived save an occasional flutter of the heart, and once a gasping sigh. But at last, just as the morning broke, the large eyes opened upon them unknowingly, as though they had been looking on great mysteries, and then dropped shut again as she moaned softly, "Oh, I am so tired!"

They said she slept, but it seemed more like death than sleep.

And suddenly, in the midst of it all, the face on the pillow seemed to fade out of Claude's vision and he found himself clinging to the foot of the bed and the doctor trying to persuade him to lie down. And some one discovered that he needed attention too. But he came to himself again soon with the sharp reality that comes always in sorrow after a moment's unconsciousness, which robs it of its pain, and insisted on coming back where he could see his wife. And the morning wore away.

Then silently there entered one of the death angel's sentinels that he posts where he may have occasion to return. Fever took up his stand beside that bed, all fire-clothed and mocking. The patient began to moan and toss and mutter of things all troublous, and out of the chaos of heart-rending sentences, that showed her husband much that otherwise he never would have known, there came one sentence again and again until it became the one sentence that the poor troubled brain could communicate:

"The pattern, the pattern, the pattern on the mount. Oh, get me the pattern on the mount!"

"What does she mean?" asked the doctor, puzzled after the hundredth attempt to quiet the restless one with answers that would set her at peace. "Had she been sewing much before she was taken ill? There is usually some little occurrence, or some big one, back of the trouble of a delirious mind, I believe," he said, "and if one is only bright enough to find out what it is, it can sometimes be removed." He looked at Claude with the light of enthusiasm for his profession in his eyes, but the husband's haggard face responded only with a hopeless compliance. He was taking his punishment bitterly.

Then Claude went out to the maid to get, if possible, some solution to the question that was troubling the patient, for the doctor felt much would be gained if her mind could be set at rest on this point and she be induced to sleep again.

Careful questioning brought out the facts from the demure maid. Yes, Mrs. Winthrop had done a great deal of sewing since when Mr. Winthrop went to Europe. She had finished all the children's clothes herself without the usual help from a seamstress, and she had made many of her beautiful gowns with her own hands. The tears flowed freely as the maid went into details. She brought different dresses from the wardrobe and showed Mr. Winthrop the exquisite needlework, the rare lace and *appliqué*, and dainty outlining of pattern in curious ribbonwork and embroidery.

Claude listened to it all helplessly, with agonized expression. He fingered the beautiful handiwork clumsily. It seemed something sacred to him. This, then, explained why no bills had come to him for all the rare garments she had worn. Then he remembered his mission.

"Did she have any patterns?" he asked awkwardly enough.

"Oh, yes, sir, a whole box full, besides those in the fashion book. I have them put by carefully," and she brought forth a large pasteboard box containing patterns of every imaginable garment a woman could put on. Her husband turned the leaves of the pile of fashion magazines without purpose. Just to touch these things that had been a part of his wife's precious life while he in his blindness had been separated from her, seemed good. (Perchance the book he held was the very one containing the letter that gave Miriam inspiration for her gigantic undertaking.) But finally he brought the box of patterns to the doctor and tried to tell him all.

They carried them to the bed and laid them out one by one and let the sick one touch them. She looked at them without interest and the paper crackled gratingly between her fevered fingers. They were the things of a life with which she seemed almost to be done. And still her lips repeated: "I want the pattern in the mount. Can no one show me where to get the pattern in the mount?"

"Is there anything in the house that she calls a 'mount'?" asked the doctor, but they shook their heads.

"It's my opinion it's a minister she needs," said the silent nurse at last. "There's something like what she's saying in the Bible, if I ain't mistaken."

The doctor's face brightened. "Surely," he said, "it must be that. Have you a minister whom she knows well?"

But Claude shook his head sadly. They had not been frequent attendants at church of late. He was unacquainted with his wife's recent attempts at identification with the church. He shrank from the strange minister who had preached the last time he was there.

"Then may I bring my brother?" said the doctor. "He is studying for the ministry and he is here on a visit. He has a lot of sense, if he is my brother, and I'd like to put him in the next room and see what he makes of all this."

Claude's heart was too heavy to care what was done. He was wrestling with the conviction that Miriam was going to die. It was traditional that dying people talked of religious things. That was what this talk of the pattern in the mount meant, of course. Strange that it had been

only the uneducated nurse who had been able to think
of it! And he sat at the foot of the bed, his haggard face
almost the counterpart of his wife's, so unceasingly did
he watch her.

They had sent for her mother to come, Claude's
mother-in-law, with her decided ways and her dainty
cameo face that Claude used to like to think Miriam's
would be like when he and she grew old together. And
she would come, and perhaps read the awful tale of his
shame and her daughter's sorrow from his eyes. He felt
that it was written there.

His mother-in-law had always liked him, and he had
returned the affection, but now she would despise him.
He shrank from that like a blow.

Then trooped back one by one the years which he and
Miriam had spent together. The little house where they
first began housekeeping—how foolish and how happy
they were there! The tiny parlor that they furnished bit
by bit as they could spare the money and how they
would go hand in hand to look at each new purchase
and he would tell her she had a new idol now to wor-
ship, and she would blush and tell him, No, she never
worshiped things that had no life.

The days when she did the work and they ate breakfast on the kitchen table to save trouble and also to save
coal! The very taste of the buckwheat cakes and syrup
that she piled upon his plate hot from the smoking grid-
dle was in his mouth. So keenly can the suffering nerves
smite back the aching heart by a sight, an odor, or a
taste.

Then there was the day when her aunt sent the lovely
little crib and its fixings, all dainty with broad blue satin
ribbons, for the expected little one that was coming to
gladden their hearts. How they had hovered over that
little nest, smoothed down the fine white coverlet, patted the little ruffled pillow and admired the softness of
the pretty blankets. And he could remember now with
what curious blending of emotions he had bent again
over that crib, alone, a few days later, and turned down
the wriggling blanket to look upon his first-born, his little Pearl, all pink and sweet and sleeping with her rose-

leaf hands tight curled and her tiny mouth set firmly as if she meant to face and conquer this world into which she had come!

That look of a madonna Miriam had given him! How it was burned into his soul now beside that changed face on the pillow, and beside it came the wraith of her as she had been that night, the last he had seen her conscious and well, her beautiful, sad face, and her reproachful eyes. Oh, horror of horrors! Oh, pity of pities! that any life could bear such punishment as his! God had no need to make a hell hereafter for such as he if this could be for all who sinned that way.

And over and over he thought it all out, the story since the day she must have known about his drive in the park. All the changes he had seen in her, and yet had not noticed at the time. The little things that she had done so carefully for his comfort on his voyage. The true meaning of her silence during his absence, the picture of the children with her own taken from the frame.

He pieced together bit by bit her carefully hidden plans, her almost superhuman effort, and its reason.

That she had had marvelous success he did not stop to wonder at. She was Miriam. No other woman could have achieved what she had, no other was worthy of it. She was peerless. So, as his old love for her grew into a new and more understanding love his sin grew in enormity, until its weight threatened to overpower him.

Then came his wonder over her treatment of Mrs. Sylvester, how she had found out, and how she succeeded in getting into the society in which that odious woman moved, and to crown all there came that last night at the Washburns', Miriam's startling beauty, and perfect self-control and the scene in the conservatory of which both he and Mrs. Sylvester had been witnesses throughout. Sometimes, for a moment, he forgot even his sorrow, to glory in the fact that Mrs. Sylvester had seen Miriam repulse the wicked man who had sought to do her harm. Almost it was worth the horror it had cost him to see those hateful lips touch his wife's, that the evil woman might know how pure, how true, his Miriam had really been.

And then he would live it over again and all the time that sweet monotonous voice would repeat:

"The pattern in the mount! The pattern in the mount!"

CHAPTER 17

•

The Ministry of Song

Adrift! A little boat adrift!
And night is coming down!
Will no one guide a little boat
Unto the nearest town?
—*Emily Dickinson.*

When Dr. Carter drove back to the Winthrop house with his brother they found Celia Lyman standing at the door, just about to enter. She had called to know how Mrs. Winthrop was.

The doctor, whose keen memory was one of the means of his success in his profession, recognized the young girl as the one who had been of much assistance the night that Mrs. Winthrop was taken ill, and according to his habit of making all things that came in his way bend to the purpose he had in hand, he asked Miss Lyman to come in a few minutes, saying he would then be better able to tell her how his patient was doing. He had it in mind that this young girl might be able to give them a clue, or at least render some help in quieting the restlessness of the sick one.

On the way to the house the doctor and his brother had talked the case over carefully. The doctor had not much religion to boast of himself, but he had all faith in his brother, and together they had arranged a little plan whereby they hoped to gain the attention of Mrs. Winthrop for a moment and get her mind quieted.

"Did you ever try music to soothe one in delirium?" asked the brother. "When I was sick in the South that winter it would put me to sleep even to hear a street hand-organ. There seemed to be something in the rhythm of sound that did all the tossing and tumbling and twisting for me, and let me rest for a few minutes. Couldn't you get her attention if some one would sing softly, some one with a sweet voice that she knew well?"

"That's a good idea, George," responded the doctor heartily; "you ought to have been a doctor yourself. It's a pity to waste yourself on the ministry."

"Won't it be as well to be a doctor of souls?" had been the answer.

Now that Doctor Carter saw Miss Lyman this conversation suddenly came back to him.

"Ask her if she can sing, George," he whispered after having introduced his brother, as he left the two in the parlor below and went upstairs.

And so it happened that a half-hour later Celia Lyman sat near the door of the room adjoining the sick-room, an old hymn book in her lap and her heart throbbing in frightened beats, ready to sing if the doctor should give her a sign to do so.

She hoped in the depths of her heart that it would not be considered necessary. She had never been so near to death before as even this, and she was afraid her voice would not respond when she tried to sing. She wondered why she had promised when that handsome stranger asked her. Of course it was nothing for her to sing that old song that she had heard a hundred times in church, and there was the music just before her; but how would her voice sound without any accompaniment but that ceaseless murmur of the monotonous voice in the next room, the voice of the woman whom she had admired, and who they said was near to the awful door of death? She shuddered as she thought of her loveliness in the beautiful gown she wore when she had last seen her. It seemed impossible that one who but a few days before was so full of life and the brightness of the world should now be all but within that mysterious shadow.

From where she sat she could catch a glimpse now and then of the bowed head and shoulders of Mr. Winthrop. She kept her face the other way. It was terrible to see deep grief in a man. She remembered how his eyes had watched his wife every time she had seen him, and girl-like she had woven of her fancies a cord of tender romance binding these two wedded souls together. All these things did not make it easier for her to sing.

When Mr. Carter first asked her if she would sing if she were needed, she had begged him not to speak of it, and shrank from going upstairs even, but when she looked into the calm eyes of the stranger and saw that he was in earnest about it, and that he expected her to be as ready to sacrifice as he would be, her pretty color came and went, and before she knew it she had consented to try. She did not like to say "No" any more than she liked to do what she was asked. But finally, with trembling heart, she followed them upstairs and took her seat with the old hymn book. She had hoped very much that no music would be found and she might have that for an excuse, but the maid at last produced from the nursery bookcase an old hymn book and the young minister had found the hymn he was looking for, and now he had gone into the sick-room and left the door ajar.

She could see Mr. Winthrop raise his head and bow as the minister came toward the bed. She could see the hopeless droop of his mouth, the heavy sadness of his eyes.

Mr. Carter stood a moment looking into the restless eyes that did not notice him, and then he said quite clearly, so that Celia could hear every word in the other room:

"I know the pattern in the mount. I can get it for you, my friend."

The low muttering ceased for a minute and the hollow eyes turned upon the speaker.

"What is the pattern in the mount?" said the high, unnatural voice. "Give me the pattern in the mount."

"Jesus Christ is the pattern in the mount," answered the clear voice once more, every word spoken as one would speak to a very little child. "And he has sent you a message to-day. He wants you to put your work away and rest."

"But I can't; I spoiled it all. My life is all cut up and it won't fit that pattern. I can't get any more to begin over again."

The restless head began once more and the low moaning that struck such terror to the hearts of the watchers.

"Jesus will make it new again if you will just rest in him. You are tired, you know, and he wants you to rest. Listen!"

The doctor gave the signal and Celia, with fluttering heart that almost threatened to choke her, sang:

> " 'Come unto me, ye weary,
> And I will give you rest.'
> Oh, blessed voice of Jesus,
> Which comes to hearts opprest!"

Then, with slight pause, she went on:

> "Just as I am, without one plea,
> But that thy blood was shed for me,
> And that thou bid'st me come to thee,
> O Lamb of God, I come!"

Celia's trembling voice ceased.

The eyes of the sick woman had kept themselves fixed upon the strange young man in a kind of wondering joy, but as the music died away she showed signs of restlessness once more.

"Now," said the clear voice commandingly again, "if you will shut your eyes and go to sleep till you are stronger, then, when you are well enough, I will tell you all about the pattern in the mount. Now, just lie still and listen."

She let him lay her hands down straight upon the white bedcover and obediently closed her eyes with the faint shadow of a smile, and Celia, her courage growing with her need, sang on:

> "Just as I am, and waiting not
> To rid my soul of one dark blot,
> To thee, whose blood can cleanse each spot,
> O Lamb of God, I come!"

On through the rest of the hymn she sang, her voice growing low and tender.

The doctor, coming up behind, with perspiration standing on his brow and the tears in his kind eyes, whispered quickly: "Don't stop for anything till I tell you. Sing on, sing something, sing anything."

And Celia, feeling as if she were a part of a great life-saving machine that was wound up and could not stop, sang on. There were three other hymns on the same page set to the same music, tender, beautiful words. She sang them all, her instinct telling her to make her voice gradually softer, and at last the nurse whispered, "He says you may stop," and Celia went downstairs, threw herself into a cozy corner, buried her face in the pile of cushions and cried as if her heart would break.

It was so that Mr. Carter found her a little later when he came down. She tried to smooth her rumpled hair and wipe the tears from her pretty face as she sat up quickly on his entrance. But he came over toward her eagerly, the light of a pleasant comradeship in his eyes.

"She is quiet now," he said with a glad ring. "Your singing soothed her wonderfully. God has given you a rare gift in your voice."

Then, noticing for the first time her tear-stained face, he said anxiously:

"It has been a great strain upon you. Of course it would be. She was your dear friend, you said."

Out into the sunshine they went, those two, who had never met before until that morning, and whom God had brought together in a bit of task for him, and talked and walked into a new world all their own.

"Oh, but I'm afraid you are mistaken about me," said Celia softly when she could get her breath to speak. "I am not—I don't know about these things. I am not—" she hesitated for a word.

"You don't mean you are not a Christian?" the young man asked anxiously. He had been so sure he detected the sympathy in her voice as she sang. He thought no one could sing like that without knowing the meaning of the words.

"Oh, no," said Celia, relieved; "I'm a Christian, I suppose. That is, I'm a member of the church. I joined when I was a little girl and all my Sunday-school class were joining. Mother thought I was too young and maybe I was. I'm not very good. I never heard anybody talk as you've done this morning and I never went where there was any trouble before. I couldn't do what you did and I didn't think I could do what I did. Oh, isn't is awful that everybody has to die?"

Her face turned gray in the sunshine and she shivered visibly.

"Yes, if that were all," the young man answered solemnly; "but when you think of eternity and heaven it would be more awful if we couldn't die, if we had to go on living in this world where trouble and sin are everywhere."

"But sin and trouble are not everywhere. This is a lovely world, the one I live in. I have been in society where there isn't any of that. I suppose of course there is sin and trouble among wicked people, and probably it is just as well for those to die and get out of it. But take for instance Mrs. Winthrop. She has a lovely little home and charming children and a husband who adores her. The last time I saw her, the night she was taken ill, she was at one of the most conservative gatherings to be found in this city. She has the *entrée* among the nicest people now, and she has perfect taste in dress. It is so dreadful for her to be in danger of dying. I think dying is cruel!"

"But sin and trouble are in the world even though they have not touched you," spoke the young man tenderly. He longed to strike an answering chord in the soul of this beautiful girl. He had come from among earnest Christian workers to visit his brother and he found the world about him chilly for his warm enthusiasm.

"I come from a recent college settlement work. I could take you to homes where little children are crying for bread and mothers are working from day to day for a few pennies to buy it, and because there is not enough for all they work on without, and give the crying, unsatisfied children their share. I could show you deathbed after deathbed where souls go out into darkness that is not broken by any whisper of the light that Jesus can give."

Celia looked up at the glowing face as he walked beside her, and thought that she knew how the face of a saint looked. And yet he was only a plain young man doing his Master's work with the fervor of a consecrated spirit.

Celia Lyman took no account of the length of the walk as she listened with absorbing interest to the story of the young man's work in the slums, and of the Christian work that a band of his college men were carrying on. It opened a new world to her, a world that appealed to her and invited her, while it yet repulsed her.

Long after the others were asleep in the Lyman home that night Celia sat by her window looking up at the stars and thinking. And the still stars answered her with their unerring steadiness that there was another world than the one of laughter and pleasure in which she had been living, and there might be more earnest living yet, even for her.

Then she knelt beside her bed and tried to pray, but the only words that would come were, "O Lord, don't let me die—not till I'm good."

And thus the task she had performed for another that day was bringing its good to her own soul, for Celia Lyman's prayers had of late been few and far between.

CHAPTER 18

•

An Unwelcome Visitor

A worthless woman, mere cold clay,
    As all false things are; but so fair,
She takes the breath of men away
Who gaze upon her unaware.
        —*Elizabeth Barrett Browning.*

The almost solemn hush that pervaded the pretty reception room of the Winthrop home where even the palms seemed to hold up warning fingers to be still, affected the beautiful woman who entered with almost a chill of dread.

Just why Mrs. Sylvester had finally decided to call and inquire concerning Mrs. Winthrop it is not easy to say. First of all, it was because she never liked to be balked in anything she undertook, and she had sense enough to see that the situation as it stood at present was against her. It was not altogether that she disliked to lose an admirer. That was unpleasant, certainly, and she knew she had all but lost. But to lose him and know that he held her in light esteem was worse. Her pride was involved and her pride was her main virtue. She had lost many an admirer by quietly turning him down when he became troublesome, and had not felt discomfort thereby, because she was assured that he would go off in some corner and dream for a little while of her beauty and grace, and sigh over the impossibility of ever possessing her, and then forget gradually; but always she would remain a pleasant picture to be thought of when alone, smoking, or when by and by the wife of his choice should annoy him in any way, as inevitably she would.

But Claude Winthrop had by no means reached the point when he was troublesome. To tell the truth he had been hard to win. From amusing herself with him one evening as a business acquaintance of her husband's she had gone on to admire and then to try to win his admiration. It had played no small part in the affair that Claude Winthrop had taken her for a pure and true woman. She had played well the part of innocence, had used her lovely eyes to advantage, and felt a thrill of exultation the first time when she succeeded in catching his eyes upon her in admiration. Her own had dropped modestly at first and then been raised shyly with a lovely sweep of color over face and neck as she had let him see a little, just a very little, of an answering admiration in them.

Of course he was not rich nor great, but then what did that matter for a married woman? She was not after position, and she was not afraid of hurting her own because she knew well how to plan her campaign so that her meetings with him would not be under any prying eyes.

It had been a long time before she had been able to win more from him than that look of admiration, but all the more earnestly had she tried, because that fact gave the affair the nature of a young, forbidden, first love, and it was worth while to win when the odds were great.

If she had made the advances they had been so delicately and naturally made that he had not suspected, and in his private conferences with his conscience during those first days when it had not been lulled to sleep, he had blamed himself, not her.

Gradually she had let him suspect what was really the truth, that her marriage was not one of love, but this was done in such a way as to leave him free to suppose that she was very unhappy over it, whereas it had been a marriage of her own planning, and in whose achievement she had secretly exulted much. It was a marriage that gave her all she wanted and left her free to be ad-

mired by whom she would. And then the pity that is
akin to love and put her hands over the eyes of his conscience while he had given that kiss of comfort—that
kiss that now he would have given worlds to call back to
him. The kiss that was his wife's and that he had thrown
away.

The beauty of his wife and her grace and success had
maddened Mrs. Sylvester into vowing she would win in
spite of everything. But strongest of all now was the fact
that she was at the point where, if she could have won
Claude Winthrop, she would be willing to leave her husband and home and everything she counted worth
while in this world, for with what heart she had she
loved him better than she had ever loved any man before. His touches upon her fingers had been all too few,
his one kiss she treasured beyond the many she had received from others.

And now it seemed that even as her rival was fallen
she was going to lose. If she would save the situation it
must be done before the enemy died, if die she did.
Mrs. Sylvester, riding toward the Winthrop home had
allowed herself for one moment to think of the possibility of what might be if Miriam should die, and her
face had softened, but only with selfishness.

And she sat down in all her elegance in the carefully
wrought reception room while she waited for Claude to
come down, as she had requested.

With cold, critical look she let her eyes rove from one
object to another, and admitted to herself that it had all
been well done though there had evidently been a
pitiful lack of money to carry out the plan.

Then she heard heavy footsteps and collected her fac-
ulties for the next act in the tragedy which she had
willed to play.

Claude Winthrop stood before her, the dull, agonized
expression of the sick room not yet faded from his face.
His eyes were heavy with loss of sleep, his collar was
awry, and he wore no tie. His hair was tumbled carelessly as though it had been smoothed with his fingers
on the way down. His caller wondered if he had not
seen her card nor known who it was that wished to see

him. She had never seen him careless in his dress before, but somehow, so perverse is human nature, he seemed all the more interesting to her because he made a sight so unfamiliar. And yet, with her cool consideration, she decided that it would not be pleasant to have a man around the house looking like that, if one were married to him.

He stood looking at her bewildered for a moment as she advanced to meet him, her delicately gloved hand outstretched to greet him, her voice sweet and sympathetic. But his hands were in his pockets, and he gripped to the lining and kept them there. The delicate little rose leaf of a hand, clad in gloves so soft as to be like a baby's skin, and so exquisitely perfumed as to leave the impression of the warm touch of a flower, that she had counted so much upon, was held out in vain. Claude looked at it as though it had been a poisonous reptile, and as she spoke the scorn grew in his eyes.

"Claude, poor fellow, I have been so sorry for you," she murmured. "I have waited from day to day in breathless eagerness to hear news. At last I could stand it no longer and came to see. How is she? She was so beautiful; I know how hard it has been for you; I do not blame you for the cruel things you said to me that night. I had a hard task and an unnecessary one, but I have felt it, oh, I have felt it these days——" There were tears in her eyes now, she had those weapons well trained and could call them ever at a moment's notice, and Claude's attitude showed her that if she would keep any influence for herself in future she must act well her part now. "I want you to forgive me for what I felt I ought to tell you about her that night. I felt I could not stand it if she should die——"

She paused to bury a well-suppressed sob in her fine handkerchief, and Claude spoke in cold deliberate tones. He was looking at her as he might have looked at the devil who had come to take him to the place of eternal punishment.

"And so it is you!" he said, scorn in his voice, "and you

have dared to follow here, and at this time! Well, I have been a fool and worse, I know, and my punishment has begun, and is perhaps none too great for me, but so long as it is in my power to prevent, it shall not include further friendship with such as you!"

Then he turned and walked out of the room and up the stairs with head erect and eyes shining with a desperate flame of anger.

Mrs. Sylvester had been prepared for almost anything, but not for this. She had never seen Mr. Winthrop any other than a perfect gentleman. She had presumed much upon this fact. She felt sure she could make him hear her out, and was reasonably certain of the final impression she would leave. But to have him go in this way was baffling beyond endurance. She bit her lip at his insolence and with rising anger declared that if she could not bring him to his senses she would at least have her revenge. Was not his position in the business world dependent upon her husband's word? How easy it would be to give a hint, a suggestion, a mere shadow of what had been this man's attentions to herself—and too, without in the least implicating herself—and her husband would fly into a mighty passion. The gleam of revenge, the malicious gleam, grew in her eyes as she looked about for some means of conquering this embarrassing situation. She must call him back for a moment if it were but to suggest this thought to him. Quickly she stepped outside the door and closing it, rang the street bell.

"Will you say to Mr. Winthrop that I have forgotten one most important thing and have come back to tell him? I will detain him but a moment." This was the message she sent by the servant when she appeared, and once more this persistent woman seated herself in the parlor.

If she had not been so wrapped about with a sense of self and her own purposes she would have felt that a hush of expectancy was pervading the very house itself, the hush of solemn crisis.

Into the chamber above, where death waited to claim

his victim, where the eyes of the watchers were turned in quiet sorrow upon that white face on the pillow, and where the only sound that could be heard was the faint breathing that had come to have so portentous a sound, came her message, borne by the troubled, reluctant maid who hesitated at the door.

Claude, kneeling in his old place at the foot of the bed, his head dropped upon his folded arms, did not see the maid at the door, nor hear her half-whispered, "Mr. Winthrop, please sir—"

His mother-in-law, who had come but a few hours before, motioned the maid to her and listened to the message. She glanced at Claude, saw the agony of his very attitude, and set her determined lips. He should not be disturbed now. Her own sorrow was a thing to be expected and accepted. Claude's was different. She knew what it would be, for had she not lost her husband in her youth?

She left the place beside her daughter's pillow and went with swift, determined step out of the door and down the stairs.

Her prim black silk and soft lace, her fine silver hair and cameo face, lit by eyes that needed no spectacles to see the minutest detail in the face of the woman she had come to cow, dawned upon Mrs. Sylvester in wonder.

"You surely cannot know that you are calling my son from the bedside of his dying wife?" she said in clear unflinching tones and fixing her piercing eyes upon the visitor fearlessly.

"Oh, I beg pardon, it was merely a matter of business," said Mrs. Sylvester sweetly, the while her soul raged within her at the way things were going after all. "I did not mean to intrude, of course. I had not heard that Mrs. Winthrop was so ill."

Mrs. Hammond's fine patrician face trembled with dignity as she cut short the voluble words.

"You will do us a favor by leaving us to ourselves at present."

And there was nothing left for Mrs. Sylvester but retreat, but as she rode away in her luxurious carriage she planned a revenge as cruel as it was sweet to her baffled heart.

CHAPTER 19

•

Getting Toward the Pattern

I was tired yesterday, but not to-day,
I could run and not be weary,
This blessed way;
For I have His strength to stay me,
With His might my feet are shod.
I can find my resting-places
In the promises of God.

—*A. C. S.*

The slow minutes dragged themselves into hours. The watchers never knew when the dark fell outside and the lights were turned on.

The doctor had taken off his overcoat and did not look as if he intended to go away again. In the next room his brother waited in the dark, for it might be there would be need for him, at least so the doctor thought. The family had not been told that he was there. Somehow the doctor always felt more hope of any desperate case when he knew his brother was near by praying, for that his brother would pray he felt sure. Though Doctor Carter did not pray himself, he sometimes took comfort in the fact that his brother did.

No one had told Claude Winthrop that the moment of the crisis was near at hand, but he seemed to know it, and his quivering heart waited for the blow hour after hour and shrank at every sound or change in the patient.

Yes, she was slipping away from him into the shadows with that awful cloud of estrangement between them and no opportunity to make it right before she went. He

143

hardly looked for any recognition from her. It was more than he dared hope. And if it came, what could he say? Could he call, "Forgive me!" down into the shadows of the valley and hope to get even an answering gleam of forgiveness from her eyes, the dear eyes that had spoken so eloquently to him in days that were gone?

Then suddenly the doctor, who with finger on the pulse had been hovering near the bed, warned them all to silence with cautioning hand, and the eyes of the sick one opened and looked upon them intelligently and her own clear voice said:

"I have seen Jesus and he is going to help me make it all over according to the pattern."

Then she smiled upon them and slept once more.

Claude remained as he had been, looking at her face. It had come then and gone, the moment which he had waited for, half hoping, yet with fear. And now it was over and the blackness was shutting about him once more. What she had said, though in so natural a tone, was something he could never understand. It showed that she had already entered a world where he did not belong. He did not doubt that the end was in sight and that this was the last word she would ever speak in the world.

He noted not the swift departure from the room of all but doctor and nurse nor the silent preparations for the night. Dazed and heavy-hearted, he followed the doctor, as he drew him away. He scarcely took in the meaning of the words, spoken low and with a ring of triumph out in the hall, "Mr. Winthrop, she will live." The words did not seem to convey their ordinary meaning to his brain. He had it firmly fixed in his mind that she would die, and he answered the kind doctor with a patient smile that showed he did not take the joyful news for truth.

"She will live, I tell you, man! The crisis is past! I hardly dared hope it would turn out so, but now I feel sure. If all goes well to-night we shall begin to go uphill instead of down. Now the next thing is for you to get a good sleep."

He made Claude lie down and tucked him up as he might have done with a baby and then slipped away, sighing to himself, "Poor fellow. He hardly understands yet. The strain has been hard on him. I wouldn't have imagined he was that sort of man."

Claude Winthrop had been passive in the hands of the doctor, but he had no idea of going to sleep. Sleep, thought he, was a thing that would never visit his weary brain again. But nature was stronger than his intentions. Placed in a relaxed position, it was not many minutes before he sank into unconsciousness, and it was not until morning was high in the world that he woke once more to the heavy burden that he carried.

For the first moment he could not remember how he came in that room nor anything that had happened. Then he concluded that his wife must be gone, else they would not have brought him away. But he saw beside him the doctor, smiling, and he knew that he would not look like that if all were over. Gradually there came to his memory the doctor's words of the night before, and a light broke over his face. He looked into Doctor Carter's eyes anxiously to read if the hope was still there.

"Doing well," he nodded reassuringly. "All she needs now is perfect quiet and perfect nursing. She will not need you for a while. She must stay, if possible, in a quiescent state. There must be no talking, no excitement. Nothing to remind her of life, or in her weak state she may have a relapse. You'd better rest yourself completely for a few days. You have been through a heavy strain. I'm going to take you in charge or we'll have a case of nervous prostration before we know it."

The doctor might have talked in a foreign tongue for all that Claude heard of what he said. His mind could take in but one thing and that was that Miriam would live. He must adjust himself to that before there was room for anything else.

His impulse was to go at once to his wife and make his full confession, for he shrank from the burden of it no longer, but gradually his common sense and the doctor's words asserted themselves. There was then hope, but he must be patient and wait for the burden to be removed, days, perhaps weeks.

After the doctor went out he lay still and listened to

the distant hum of the city outside, the sound of the world to which they had come back, he and Miriam, to live over again the life they had failed to live aright. No, not they, but he. Miriam had been all right. Miriam had been true through all. To him now came the picture sharp and clear of the way she had struck the senator in the conservatory. He had not heard all he said, but he had seen the kiss. He gloried in Miriam's righteous wrath. He had not been true to her, but she had been absolutely true to him, and that in spite of knowing of his weakness.

Hour after hour he reviewed the story, taking up details he had not remembered before, and always coming up against the blank wall of his own defenseless weakness—no, *sin*, for that was the name by which he had learned to call his own conduct.

By and by he slept again, but now came dark dreams to trouble him, and always the face of his wife, cold, sad, averted from him. He woke with the sweat of agony on his brow.

They let him into the sick-room but seldom now, and only when she was asleep. He must not come near her or touch her or do anything to take her out of that restful world into which she had slipped. It was their only hope for her recovery that she might remain untroubled by anything, not even the joy of seeing her loved ones, until her heart had grown a little stronger and she was able to bear emotion of any kind.

The husband hovered about the door of the sick-room, haunting the halls like a gaunt spectre and asking anxiously for any news of the nurses or the doctor as they passed. He seemed to feel it a part of his just punishment that at this time, when his place should have been close beside his dear wife, he should be thus shut away from her, more shut away than he had ever been in his life before. He grew almost to hate the nurses whose presence kept her he loved so secluded from his view.

Doctor Carter pitied him from the depths of his heart, but he dared not let him come into the presence of his wife yet, lest his haggard face should startle her and she become aware of her own serious condition. She was entirely herself now when awake, and seemed to be perfectly content to lie still and do as she was bid. She had not asked for any one, and did not seem to care for anything but just to lie and rest. The time had not come to rouse her from this state. Until then her husband must wait and be patient.

But Doctor Carter spoke to his brother about it.

"I wish, George, you would see what you can do at doctoring the soul of that man if you know anything about the business," he said, one afternoon as he came out from the house to the carriage where his brother was waiting for him; "he needs something to soothe him a little. If religion is worth anything at all it ought to be able to do that. Sometime when you're in there just see if you can't get him to talk with you. He is taking life as hard as he did last week when there was practically no hope. If he keeps on he'll break down before she gets to the point where he will be needed."

And the brother pondered in his heart what he might be able to say to this older man who seemed to be locked so firmly within his sorrow.

With Miriam the world had receded so far, and all things grown so dim, that she was a long time in coming back to the things that had been hers once more. Her memory of her illness was like some horrible journey over stormy seas, over rapids and dangerous rocks, with thunder and lightning all about, until suddenly a voice had said, "Peace, be still," and her little bark which was about to sink amid the tempest had drifted into quiet waters, where the sunlight glinted through leafy shadows, and a great peace arched over all. There was rest, deep, sweet rest. And in that haven she was content to stay.

She swallowed what they gave her obediently, and she lay and rested and forgot.

Gradually there came order out of the chaos of her mind. She did not remember the song nor the words that had been spoken to her when she was under the power of the fever, but she knew that a new influence had taken hold of her life that would make all wrongs right. To this thought she fixed her heart. She had left the problems of her life all unsolved, but they did not trouble her any more. They were in hands that knew well how to control them. Where she got this faith she did not know, did not question. That it was in her heart gave her comfort. She would not let herself think about the old troubles, as her mind grew stronger and memory, always a poor nurse, rushed in with pictures filled with old troubles. She did not question about anything. She tried as much as possible to keep from wondering how she came here and where her husband and children were.

But there came a time at last when she could no longer put by memory. She awoke one morning to find the walls of her mind all hung with pictures, fresh and vivid, of the weary way she had trod before she had found this haven. They pierced her with their darts of evil. And about three portraits her gaze lingered longest. One beautiful, scornful face crowned with golden hair, another old and wicked, topped with silver white, and a third, the face averted with indifferent aspect, with soft sweep of dark hair, and handsome, manly outlines. Ah! here was her world all back again, and whither was her peace flown?

She looked up and seemed to see a light and to hear a voice speaking to her soul: "Come unto me, and I will give you rest."

Why had that rest not meant death for her? What other rest could there be but that? And yet it had not been, and still the voice insisted, "I *will* give you rest." And gladly, gladly she took hold once more upon a faith that had come to her out of the dark of her forgotten childhood when her mother's teachings had fallen on unheeding childish ears.

There is much perplexity and sadness about whether a soul taken from this earth out of the midst of life not lived for God, and spending its last moments in delirium, can be saved. But why does not comfort come to such questioners from the thought of the power of the God who made that soul, to speak to it even in delirium? It is not strange that God should speak to one of his creatures now any more than that he spoke to Adam or to Moses.

It was in some such way that Miriam came back to life, knowing that henceforth if she lived her life at all, she must live it hand in hand with God. And thus she came to herself, feeling content to lie in God's hand, but dreading to come back to a life which had baffled her on every side.

It was then the doctor began to be uneasy. She was not gaining fast enough, but seemed to have come to a standstill.

Something more was needed to rouse her to an interest in the world and give her an object for getting well. Doctor Carter thought at once of her husband, and had decided to bring him in to see her for a few minutes, but when he went in search of him he found him with a drawn and haggard expression upon his face, so much worse than it had been during the days that had passed that he changed his mind and decided to try the children first. A woman would do more for her baby anyway than for any one else on earth.

It had been thought best that Miriam should not know that her mother was in the house yet, lest she should guess how ill she had been, therefore the grandmother had taken up her place in the nursery, to the delight of the children, who had sorely missed their mother's devotion of late.

Little Celia was brought to her mother first, and nestled down shyly beside her on the pillow, and touched the thin hand wonderingly, and the other children came and kissed her softly in awe, for her face was changed by her illness, white and almost unearthly in its beauty, and then they trooped away glad to get back to the cheer of the nursery and grandmother's stories, while Miriam lay still, feeling that she had drifted out away from even her children, that they had learned to do without her while she was ill, and that she was not needed back among them now.

On the whole the doctor's experiment had not succeeded so well as he had hoped. He sat down and studied the problem in perplexity. To have brought his patient out from the shadow of death thus far and then to see her slip slowly back again was more than he could endure.

"George," said he impatiently, as his brother came into the office, "why don't you pray this thing out for me? What's the use of prayer if you can't work a miracle now and then?"

And the result of that conference was that once more George Carter stood beside that bed and spoke.

He came in quietly as if his coming were an every-day affair.

"I came to see you once before when you were so ill, Mrs. Winthrop," he said, smiling pleasantly. "You don't remember me, I suppose? You were troubled about the 'pattern in the mount,' and I promised to tell you more about it when you were stronger. Would you like to hear it now?"

Miriam's face lit with a half-smile of remembrance.

"I heard a sermon once—" she said and paused. Speech seemed long and hard to her yet.

"Yes, and you were so tired and were troubled that you had not made your life according to the pattern?"

She nodded understandingly.

"I told you then that Jesus wanted you to rest. I bring you another message to-day. It is this, 'Be *strong* in the Lord.' He wants you to get well and begin to live after the pattern that he has set for you. You need not be troubled that you think you have spoiled it all. He will make that right. When you are strong you will find the pattern with careful directions in his book. Now will you obey the message and get well?"

Wonderingly she answered, "Yes." It seemed to her that some strong angel had been sent down to speak to her and give her heart of life again. And she was near enough yet to the other world not to be much amazed over it.

The young man knelt beside the bed and closed his eyes:

"Dear Lord," he said, "help this child of thine to get strong for thee, and show her how to follow thee. For Jesus' sake."

Then he was gone, and Miriam lay thinking of it all, and in her heart there grew again determination to make the fight anew, this time with the God of battles on her side, and win.

CHAPTER 20

•

In the Devil's Grip

Fool! All that is, at all,
Lasts ever, past recall;
Earth changes, but thy soul and God stand sure.
            —*Robert Browning*.

Claude Winthrop had paid little attention to his business
since the night his wife was taken ill. He had sent a message down to the office to the effect that his wife was in a
serious condition, and that he could not leave home.
Twice the private secretary had been out to consult him
about some important affair that he only was familiar
with, but beyond that and friendly notes of sympathy
from different men in the house—which he had scarcely
read—he had heard nothing. It had not seemed strange
to him that things were going on just the same without
him, nor had he stopped to think that the notes he had
received from the heads of the firm had been curt and
formal.

He knew that he had left affairs in such shape that the
man just below him could manage everything until he
went back, and beyond that he had not troubled himself.
What was business at such a time as this?

And then, three days after the crisis had passed and
the little world of their friends came to know that
Miriam was better, and ere he himself had as yet been
able to move out from under the shadow that had settled upon him, there came a letter which brought him
suddenly to his senses.

It was on the afternoon that Doctor Carter intended to
take him in to see his wife that the letter had come. He

picked it up from the desk where the maid had placed it after the two o'clock delivery and read it, idly at first, and then starting to his feet, read it over again trying to understand the words. They danced before his eyes and would not stand still for him to understand. But at last he comprehended. It was a firm but courteous dismissal from the business house where but yesterday he had supposed he was in a fair way to become second only to the head in a few years, and perhaps, if all went well, even one of the heads by and by.

How had his ambitions crumbled at his feet? How was he fallen? What could it mean? Was it a dream? What had brought it about? They surely had not dismissed him for the brief absence when his wife hung between life and death. They were good men. They would not do that. He must go down and see about it at once. There was some mistake. They had sent the letter to the wrong man or some clerk had blundered. He started to his feet and found that he was trembling from head to foot. He must not go in this way. He must steady himself. This long nightmare of sickness and trouble had upset him. But he must set this thing straight at once. Why, where would he be if he lost his business connection? What would Miriam and the children do? How precious had they become! How terrible it would be if this were true, but of course it could not be. It was some mistake.

Just then a maid tapped on the door and handed him a special delivery letter. He frowned at the interruption, signed his name in the book, and sat down impatiently to see what the letter contained.

It was a dainty envelope that bore the large blue stamp, and filled the room about it with a subtle fragrance that carried a hateful memory with it. It was the fragrance of lilies of the valley. His heart stabbed him that the perfume of his wife's wedding flowers should have power to bring a hateful memory. But he tore open the thick envelope and read, his eyes growing dark with anger and understanding:

DEAR CLAUDE:—I am sorry for you in your humiliation. I would have done something for you if I dared, but my husband was very angry. But though I have cause to be angry with you, still I forgive you, and if you will come to me I will yet put you in the way of something far better than the position which you occupied.

He read no further, but tearing the letter in tiny bits put it in the flames of the fireplace until every atom was consumed. Then he rose and began to pace the floor. He knew now whom he had to thank for his dismissal. This, then, was her revenge!

It was just at this point that the doctor looked in and changed his mind about taking Claude to see his wife.

And while the angel of peace was taking up his abode with the wife, the husband wrestled with the adversary.

All that long afternoon he paced his room inside locked doors. He did not go down to the office as he intended. He knew now that it would be of no use. If Mr. Sylvester had spoken the word it was final. There was no appeal from that. And Mrs. Sylvester had arranged it so. He followed carefully every thread of evidence. Things that he had said and done and forgotten came up now to haunt him. The case was against him. And what could he do or say? He could not go to Mr. Sylvester and say that his wife's insinuations were false, because there was enough of truth for their foundation to make that impossible. He could not tell the man that the fault had been the woman's in the first place because that would be as useless as it was pitiful, for after all, would it better his case to say that he had been weak enough to be led by a woman into temptation? And how well he knew that that woman could make herself appear as pure and unsullied as a star in the heavens. He was caught in a net. He was bound hand and foot. It was too late to even try to extricate himself. And why had she done it? Was it her cruel desire to subjugate, that she still wished to keep him a slave to herself and so, though having shown him her power over him, yet show him her tenderness by offering help just now when she knew his extremity? Or did she really care for him? He recalled looks and actions more meaningful than mere coquetry. How they would have made his foolish heart throb in some of the days gone by to have recognized what they meant. But now it was a sort of fear of her that filled him. She was determined to have his love, and it seemed that he was powerless to keep her from it. What had he left but to go to her for help—or let Miriam and the children suffer?—and what would that be but to begin again the double life which had caused him so great misery during the past weeks?

Then it was given to him at last to look into the open mouth of the horrible pit of wickedness into which his feet had almost slipped beyond reclaim. He saw things as they were. He called things by their names. His own soul appeared cringing before his sharpened judgment, all blackened with dishonor. And in that lurid place where abode the evil thoughts and careless actions of his past days, each one an evil spirit come to haunt him, he thought he was going insane. What ugly creatures were these that menaced all hope of peace, these little evil-faced imps that mocked at him as if they had a right? Was it possible that they were his own thoughts? Had he really entertained such creatures and taken pleasure in them when they had appeared as angels of light?

Cold sweat stood upon his forehead and he pressed his burning eyeballs for relief from pain. Almost he seemed to see a vision of eternal fires prepared for such writhing souls as his who had dared to fashion a torture so exquisite for a soul so pure as Miriam's.

And he had ventured to hope for a reconciliation. He, blackened as he was with the evil he had harbored in his thoughts! He to expect once more to touch her sweet hand, and have the honor of pressing her precious lips against his own dishonored ones—his lips that had promised and had not performed, his lips that had deliberately been untrue to her! He to think ever to have her look with clear and trustful gaze into his eyes with eyes of love!

The knocks that came to his door from time to time, the call to dinner, the messages that came to the house, made no more impression upon his mind than if they had been the moaning of the wind outside. At first he only answered that he was busy, but as he became more and more absorbed he did not respond at all, nor even lift his head from where it had sunk upon his arms on his desk.

Life in the future looked too black for him to face. He seemed to have reached the end of all things for himself. Now and again he would bring himself to consider the possibility of going to Mrs. Sylvester and taking the business chance she offered for Miriam's sake, but the thought of bringing help to Miriam through the one who had caused her so much sorrow was intolerable. Then he would try to consider what he should do. It was useless to think of attempting to get something else in that same city with a tarnished character. Neither could he ever face his wife with all this upon him. They would be better off without him. He was now but a sorrow and humiliation to them, his wife and his children. Through sharpened memory he knew as clearly how Miriam had felt about his relations to Mrs. Sylvester as though he had been able to read her heart. It was like looking at his shameful self through eyes that saw as the eyes of God see.

There was nothing for him but that horrible torture into which he had been looking, or the worse torture of going on with life.

It had grown dark in his library now, and the room felt chilly. Some one had turned the heat away from the room, but he had not noticed it before. If they should find him lying here to-morrow cold and dead, they would hide it from Miriam until she was better, and when she was strong enough to hear it, it would be to her but a fit ending for the sorrowful story she had begun many months back. He could never hope now to win back her love and favor again. Even a "clean breast" of it could never undo the past. He would not even be able to support her as he had done of late, and there would be disgrace too, attached to him, which would be harder for her to bear. If he ended it all to-night there would at least be pity. There was always pity for one who went out of life by his own hand. Perhaps they would say he had lost his mind through worry over his

wife's illness. And perhaps he had! He felt as if it were
gone.

Only one thing was clear. He saw it shining before
him now out of the darkness of the room; though its
cruel metal form was shut away in a locked drawer, it
gleamed with swift and irrevocable relief.

He struck the light to find the key of the drawer. The
key had been put away from other keys because Miriam
was afraid of the wicked instrument of death. It had
been one of the purchases of his younger days when the
possession of a revolver was synonymous with man-
hood. He had argued that it was necessary to have one
to protect his family in case of burglars, and he had
proudly slept with it under his pillow until in deference
to Miriam, it had gone, first to a high shelf in the closet
near the bed, then to this secret drawer, where it had
stayed. For as the little ones had entered their home and
his fatherhood had grown more deeply protective he
had feared the revolver himself, lest the children should
by mistake play with it some day.

It was not loaded. He had cleaned it carefully and un-
loaded it, and showed it to Miriam one day when she
was worried and fearful of it, and had put it where he
had scarcely looked at it since.

There was a sort of morbid fascination in handling it
now. Clearly, out of the shadows of the room came the
picture of his wife as she had sat there sewing while he
put it away. Ah, she never dreamed how it would be
with them both when he should take it out as he was
doing now, and load it that he might end his own
wretched existence with it.

And after? Yes, there might be more to life than what
appeared, but it could scarcely be worse than was his
here. He did not think of it. It seemed to him that in
ending his life he was at least showing his own remorse
for the folly that had made of their happy home a place
of misery.

Slowly, deliberately, he opened the box containing the
tiny things that would bring swift healing to his sick soul
and wipe out all this horror. He was as calm about load-
ing that revolver as if he intended to kill a squirrel in-

stead of himself. And when his work was complete he carefully closed the drawer and locked it again and put all the little articles on his desk straight. Then he placed the cold steel to his temple, moving it carefully to the vital spot, and raised his trembling finger to the trigger.

His senses were on the alert. He knew perfectly what he was about to do. There was in his face a light of triumph. He saw the end in view and blessed relief from the terrible self-condemnation.

The house had been still for a long time. He realized it too, with all the rest that came before him now in this one clear moment of vision. He felt the silence of the street and all the neighborhood, in the anticipation of the loud report that would presently ring out. He was glad the library was so far from Miriam's room. She would not be disturbed by the sound. They would keep all quiet for her sake, and he would be gone!

His finger was touching the trigger now. In an instant more all would be over.

Suddenly in the stillness of the room there came a sound and the revolver dropped from the nerveless fingers of the man standing upon the threshold of another world.

CHAPTER 21

•

After the Storm, Peace

> Behind the dim unknown,
> Standeth God within the shadow, keeping watch
> above his own.
>
> —*James Russell Lowell.*

Strange what creatures of habit and memory we are! An odor will carry us back over scores of years into scenes we have not thought of for many a long day. A touch will set vibrating in us chords that we thought dead. The sight of the curve of a cheek, like that of a lost loved one, will bring back to us old impulses and change our plans in a moment, while a sound will call us into sudden action and set every nerve a-throbbing.

The sound which broke the stillness of that room of agony and brought Claude Winthrop from a suicide's act to one of frightened ministration was commonplace enough to have passed with other sounds of the night, and yet one that had never lost its power of striking fear to his heart.

It was the hoarse, shrill bark of croup, and the sound came from the room overhead, where his baby, Celia, slept in her little white crib, close by the register, whose flue was also connected with the library register.

The cough was hoarse enough to have alarmed one less preoccupied than Claude, but it came to him with the sharp arrow of memory. He saw himself as he was those few short years gone by, when that sound had first broken upon his terrified ear and their first child struggled for breath. He could feel again, as he felt then, the

impossibility of fastening the buttons of his clothes with
his trembling fingers and the frightful sense of the agony of time that would have to pass before he could get
the doctor there. He could see Miriam white and frightened, with the tears streaming unheeded down her
cheeks and her long hair falling about her white gown,
as she frantically searched the index of an old medical
book her mother had given her, along with a recipe book
and the Bible for their first setting-up of housekeeping.
They had recognized croup at once as the much-talked-
of terror, which, like death, one hears of and dreads but
yet never really expects to come his way.

Claude's first realization when he heard that sound
was that the last time he had heard it was the night he
arrived home from Europe. Then the mother had been
there and the cough had not been severe. Now the
mother was lying asleep, weak and frail, unable to go to
the little one, just having crept back from the dark valley
of the shadow. And the father, the other one upon
whom the little one depended, had been hovering in
that valley too, but by his own wish and cowardly purpose.

It was almost strange that the weary brain, which during the day and evening had been subjected to so many
varying sensations, and the eyes that had looked so
clearly into his past life and his present, had yet strength
left to look in the face the cowardly portrait of himself as
it appeared after the last two hours in his library.

This all went through his mind like a flash while he
locked the revolver away from sight, and then bounded
away up the stairs to the nursery.

The nurse had already been roused and was on her
way to the bath room for hot water. The little one sat up
in her crib crying and coughing frightfully. She held out
her hands piteously to her father and he gathered her
up, all swathed in her blankets, and held her in his arms,
the wildness melting out of his eyes and a tender light
growing there instead.

The nurse was sleepy and did not like being roused
from her slumber. Moreover, she knew in her heart that
the cause of this attack was her own carelessness for hav-

ing allowed Celia to stand in the keen draught of an open door while she flirted with the grocer's boy the day before. She worked only half-heartedly, and the father finally sent her to telephone for the doctor and himself arranged the cold compress on the struggling little throat and covered it carefully with many folds of flannel. With one free hand he lighted the alcohol lamp under the kettle of water that was always kept in the nursery for such a time of need, and soon the steam in the air and the frequent applications of the cloth wrung from cold water relieved the little girl so that she was able to speak.

She slipped a hot hand from the folds of blanket and patted his cheek feebly.

"Good, good poppie, take care Celie," came the hoarse whisper. "Dear, good poppie won't leave Celie 'lone any more?"

He assured her he would stay with her and snuggled her close to his breast, and in this safe shelter behind his little one, with the everyday domestic atmosphere about him, a great peace came into his heart. The other life, that life which he had been about to take, seemed so far away, so impossible. How could he ever have sinned with the sweetness, the purity of his little ones in his keeping?

The thoughts of the world, the struggles he had passed through during the afternoon and evening, the tortures that had been his, were all outside this little room. He could even put them from his mind. They did not belong here, where love reigned supreme.

The grandmother came frightened from her room, with a gray look about her face. She had forgotten the days when her own children were ill, and croup had taken on a new terror for her. She offered to hold Celia, but the father shook his head and held her close, and was comforted by the little hand that clung to his neck and the hoarse voice that fretted, "No, poppie keep Celie."

He held her all night long, even after the doctor had come and the disease had been controlled and the household settled to quiet.

And then was fulfilled anew that prophecy which said, "And a little child shall lead them."

Through that little sleeping girl the heavenly Father spoke to the weary, sin-sick soul of the earthly father. All the long night did he feel the love and tenderness of the infinite Fatherhood that bears with the sins and follies of his earthly children. And as a penitent child did he judge himself. And now it was not so much horror for what he had done as sorrow that filled his heart.

When morning came the little one smiled and patted his face again, and cooed gently: "Oo did stay, poppie, oo stayed wiv Celie."

They had their breakfast together on the little round white table which he had fashioned in his evening hours about Christmas time during the days of Pearl's babyhood, when money with which to buy toys was not so plentiful as of late years. He ate bites of her poached egg and toast, that she fed him, and took sips of her milk obediently, and each ate more than they would have done alone.

The other children gathered about their father with surprise and delight. The tired grandmother saw that she was not needed and retired to rest.

He let himself be taken by storm and be soothed by their fluttering hands. He reveled in their clear eyes and direct speech. He told stories of adventure and fun. He read the Mother Goose books through as many times as the young tyrants demanded, and he built houses of blocks for them to overthrow. There was nothing, even to dressing Celia's doll, that he stopped at, though the costume when finished presented a most remarkable combination.

But when at a call from the nurse he was forced to go downstairs to see about having a prescription filled for the doctor he shivered visibly. Here in the light, cheery nursery, which everywhere spoke of Miriam's presence, he had been able to forget the nightmare of the days that were passed, ending in the almost tragedy of the night before.

Cold chills crept down his back as he passed the library door, and he was glad to find it closed. It seemed as if all the evil thoughts that had visited him the previous night must be shut within the walls of that room.

And it was necessary after all for him to enter the library to get the prescription the doctor had written the day before, which must be renewed. He knew it was lying on his desk next to the letter of dismissal that had come to him. The doctor had hurried away to his lecture at the medical college to which he was already late, leaving his brother, who had kindly offered to save Claude the trouble of going out, and he stood there waiting now.

As he watched the haggard look creep into Claude Winthrop's face he prayed in his heart for some opportunity to help him and followed to the library door.

Claude was glad of his companionship. He dreaded to look about him. He breathed a sigh of relief as he remembered that he had locked the revolver out of sight the evening before. It seemed as if it could but tell the tale of his cowardice and sin if it lay there in sight.

As they entered, to Claude's fevered imagination, the shadows seemed to shrink into the corners and take the forms of all the fiendish tortures that had been here dealt out to him a few hours ago. The little gold cup on the mantel, innocent in itself, had somehow reminded him last night of the first tiny cup of tea Mrs. Sylvester had handed him when she began to weave her spell about his unsuspecting heart! There were the ashes in the grate that spoke of the partly read letter he had burned! There was the whole dreadful mistake of his life again all standing about in the pictures, the chairs, the drapery, everything that he had looked at in his march about the room. So memory uses commonplace hooks to hang our deeds upon, and we may not take them down and put them out of sight however much we try.

"I wish that I might do something more for you."

It was George Carter who spoke, wistfully, as he lingered by the door with the prescription in his hand.

Claude looked up surprised out of his absorption. It did him good to see the other man still standing there. It dispelled some of the shadows from his mind. It was like medicine to hear the sympathetic tones. His heart went out in longing for that sympathy. He liked this wholesome man whose coming seemed like some strong, life-giving breeze from the mountain-tops. It brought relief from the stagnant, humid depths of what his own nature had come to be.

The look on his face drew the younger man back to the desk again, and the two pairs of eyes met in a recognition of their brotherhood as it is given for spirit to speak to spirit without the use of words.

"I wish you could give me a prescription that would cure mistakes," said Claude earnestly, thinking of the days when he was this young man's age, and wishing he could go back to that time and begin over his life. He felt sure he could live it better in the light of all he now knew.

The light of longing came into the eyes of the young minister. "'As far as the east is from the west, so far hath *He* removed our transgressions from us!' repeated the young man reverently. "Won't that apply to mistakes too, don't you think, if we ask him?"

A hopeless sorrow settled into the face of Claude.

"It wouldn't apply to the inevitable results," said Claude hopelessly.

"God controls all results," said George Carter. "He is able to make even the result of terrible mistakes work together for good to them that love him."

"But I am not one of those," said Claude sadly.

"It is your privilege to be."

There was a great silence in the room. And all those shadows in the corners gathered about and drew together, and hovered over and behind Claude Winthrop contending for his soul. Almost they had succeeded last night. Now another Power, greater than themselves, was here. A light of hope was shining into that room.

By and by Claude broke the stillness which had been with his guest one silent prayer.

"Will you pray for me?" He spoke in husky tones.

Broken and contrite he knelt beside the same chair in which he had sat and planned to take his life. He wondered as he listened to the simple, earnest prayer that

any man could come so near to God. Ah! if he had been
like that he never could have gone so far astray.

"Father, thou knowest this man's heart. Thou knowest
his sorrow, his mistakes, his failures—" and to Claude
came a realization that God had known all the time, had
watched him when he put the revolver to his temple,
had stayed his hand by the cry of his child, had been
guarding him from himself.

One by one the evil spirits were exorcised and slunk
away from that room, forever. And in the heart of the
man bowed low before his Maker there grew a "light
that never shone on land or sea."

He gripped the hand of his guest as they arose from
their knees.

"I would give worlds," said Claude, "if I had begun
this way, as you have done."

When George Carter was gone and he was left alone
he had no more fear for the haunting memories of the
night. He could even quietly open the drawer where lay
the revolver and remove the cartridge and put it away in
safety without a shaking hand. In his heart was a great
thankfulness that he had been saved from himself and
allowed one more chance. His life that he would have
thrown away was saved and then gently given back that
he might try it over again and see if he could not better it
with God's help.

He could not see ahead. He did not know what he
should do nor how he should do it, but he knew that
whatever he did was to be done in a different way from
any that he had ever tried before, and with different
motives. And please God, if he ever stood with his life at
the mercy of a revolver again, it should be held in the
hand of another, and he would not have the regret for
his past that had held him so fast last night.

CHAPTER 22

·

Reconciliation

O heart! O blood that freezes, blood that burns!
  Earth's returns
For whole centuries of folly, noise and sin!
  Shut them in,
With their triumphs and their glories and the rest!
  Love is best.

—*Robert Browning.*

And now at last Miriam began to wonder about her husband. She searched her mind for any memory of his presence in the sick-room during her illness, but could not be sure of it. Had he then deserted her entirely? And they would not tell her of it till she was stronger!

Little by little the incidents of that last awful afternoon and evening came to her mind. She stood again upon the Sylvester doorstep and met her husband face to face. She met him at the entrance to the Washburn conservatory, and she lived over the shameful scene with the senator, and her flight, until it ended in unconsciousness at her husband's feet. Had he turned upon his heel and spurned her then before the world? He knew what the senator was. He had tried to warn her once, and she had resented it because she felt he had no right to call her to account when he was so much more at fault than she; but now she saw her own part in sinful colors. She should have been more careful. She had been so blind, and so wrapped up in her own purposes! To think that she could go against the whole world and win back her own! No, she had but brought shame and disgrace upon herself!

But God had forgiven. He would help her to begin over again, only how could she ever bear it without Claude? If only it could have been right that she should die. But there were the children. Then her new purpose came back to her, and a portion of the comfort, but she set her eyes restlessly upon the door and knew all who entered before the door was fairly open.

She would not ask one question, for if there were shame to tell and more humiliation, she did not want them to watch her bear it. It was for her and God. She kept hoping the suspense would be over, and some word would show her just how matters stood with regard to her husband, so that she might have opportunity to adjust herself to the new state of things during this resting-time when she could keep her eyes closed and shut out the world of other beings and be alone with God.

There came a night when the night nurse was suddenly taken ill. The day nurse had been going home at evening since Miriam had grown so much better. There was no one to call upon but Claude.

The nurse was too ill to hesitate long. She called Mr. Winthrop and asked him to stay with the patient for an hour or two until she should feel better. There was nothing to be done. The patient was sleeping quietly, and would probably continue to do so all night. If she should stir there was the medicine to be given, and there was water in the pitcher in the window. Mrs. Winthrop would not notice the change even if she should waken.

Then the nurse betook herself to a couch in the next room with her aching head, and Claude stole softly into the darkened room with bated breath as though he were entering a sacred temple.

It was a precious privilege, this of sitting once more beside her whom he loved better than his own life—who had been given back to him from the dead. There was a future into which he dared not look as yet, which might hold sorrow and estrangement still from her, but the present was his and she lay here for him to guard.

Silently he took his seat as though he had been asked to sit in an antechamber of heaven, and counted not the hours slow while he heard the music of her regular breathing, and blessed God with every breath that she was here alive and getting well.

How he longed to stoop and kiss the sweet brow. But no, he must never do that until she had forgiven him. And could she ever forgive him?

Her white hand lay like a lily against the whiteness of the bed covering. He knelt and reaching out one hand laid it near to hers. And by and by it crept a little nearer, till one finger touched hers.

It was like feeling warm and living the hand of one who had gone out into the land of the dead. It thrilled him with a deeper joy than even when he had touched it long ago in the rose-bordered lane where they had wandered together when first he took that hand in his and dared to hold it, and they both walked silent, neither letting the other see by look or motion what each was feeling over that hand-clasp.

When the morning broke gray and pink in the eastern window, and the heavy-eyed nurse, somewhat refreshed from her sleep, came back to take his place, he went out from that room and knelt beside his baby's crib and prayed, prayed that God might make him better and more worthy to have and keep the precious wife who had once been his so fully.

Thereafter he made a habit of stealing in at night and sending the nurse to lie down, while he watched beside the bed, and the nurse, nothing loath, obeyed.

Then he would look at the sweet face upon the pillow, softly shaded in the darkened room, and let his whole soul go out to her in a caress. And more and more he dared touch the hand that lay upon the bed beside him, to even lay his own hand closely over it as if it were a little lost, cold bird.

She never spoke nor stirred, nor awakened in the least. And so he would continue to kneel beside her till the morningtime and he knew the nurse was coming back.

And in these vigils he told her all again and again. He bitterly blamed himself, and then told her how he loved her. How the love he had given her before was as nothing to the new love that had blossomed here beside her sick-bed.

And all the time she lay there in her weakness asleep, and answered him not by so much as the fluttering of an eyelash.

His heart cried out in agony at last that he might speak to her, might roll this awful burden of confession at her feet, and let her know that in those terrible moments when he had been made to appear before her in the wrong, he had not been so very wrong as it looked; let her know that her fears were greater than the truth, and that he had not ceased to love her, but loved her in his repentance with an aching love that could never be satisfied—no, not if they should have an eternity to live and love each other.

And once when he was holding her hand close and thinking so, and praying, she drew a long, quivering sigh, and that was all. And then he moaned softly to himself, and laid his face down on the hand that lay in his so still and strengthless.

And Miriam dreamed a dream, a sweet, sweet dream. She had not dreamed the like since first her sorrow had pierced her soul. She dreamed her husband was beside her and that his hand touched hers, and she smiled in her sleep, and would not stir lest she should wake and find him gone.

Claude saw that smile, and wondered if when grown people smiled in their sleep it was because they were in pain, as nurses said of little babies in their sleep.

When the morrow came and Miriam remembered her dream she hugged it close to her heart, and all that day would not look toward the door nor listen to the nurses, lest she should hear some word that might dispel it. She longed for night to come that she might dream the sweet thing over once more. And with the memory of his touch, his loving touch once again, she forgot, as foolish, loving woman will, the misery and the shame he had brought her to bear, and found she loved him still. And from that time the portraits of the woman and of the senator began to fade in memory's gallery until they took on the natural color of the other pictures there.

Night came, and Miriam sank to sleep in a blessed anticipation which wafted her to unconsciousness like a breath from a bed of glowing poppies. Would the dream come again, or would it not?

And again it came.

The next day the doctor thought her decidedly better, and wondered if it would not be a good plan to let her husband in in daylight to have a bit of a talk with her, but she seemed so content to lie and smile and do as she was bidden that he hardly dared to break the spell yet for any experiments. His brother had told him of his conversation with the husband and he felt a little uneasy about the effect that his appearance might have on his wife. So he held his peace for one day more, and thought about it.

Miriam came to sudden consciousness that night in the midst of her dream. The dream was there in all its reality. She felt the strong hand holding hers, she knew the long supple fingers, and the smooth texture of the skin. And that was his face touching her palm, his cheek, as he used to lay it in her hand long ago. But she was awake and not dreaming. Why did the dream not go? She dared not stir, but lay there trying to make her breath come regularly as in sleep. She dared not lift her eyelids lest the dear dream should pass.

Her quivering heart reviewed all she knew of the tragedy of their lives once more, and she judged him before the bar of her soul as guilty, and yet she loved him. It stood much in his favor that he had still some love for her, for he would never lay his cheek so in her hand unless he had. 'Tis sad a woman will forgive all else save lack of love for her. And that she cannot forgive.

And then herself—she was not so worthy of his love as in the past. For had she not sinned also?—though without intention and unthinkingly. But he had a right to question her conduct with the senator. Perhaps, perhaps, there was something too, to plead on his side. Perhaps he was not all wrong or weak or wicked as she feared!

And then a drop fell on her hand, and straightway she knew it for a tear.

At once the motherhood in her, that is a part of all true wifehood, rose. A great love and pity swept over her. He was sorry. And as she would have done with a sorrowful, repentant child, she reached out arms that were suddenly made strong by love and gathered her dream to herself.

"Miriam, my darling, can you forgive?" He spoke the words brokenly. He was frightened that he had waked her, but the moment had come and she had enfolded him in her arms and his face was resting in the old place on her bosom.

Her answer was a kiss.

When the nurse came to take his place that morning she thought the glory in his face was from the rosy reflection of the eastern sky, and she blamed herself that she had slept so late.

Miriam lay with closed eyes and face turned away and apparently slept still, but the joy that glowed in her consciousness would hardly be kept within bounds.

CHAPTER 23

•

New Paths Opening

Great feelings hath she of her own,
Which lesser souls may never know;
God giveth them to her alone,
And sweet they are as any tone
Wherewith the wind may choose to blow.
                    —*James Russell Lowell.*

Dinner in the Lyman home was strictly a family affair the evening of the arrival home from abroad of Celia's only brother, and they lingered late over the dessert, enjoying the luxury of asking all the questions that one forgets to put in letters, or to answer when they are found there.

"By the way, father, have you opened up the new department in the business that you were speaking of when I left?"

"Well, no, we haven't," answered the father passing his cup for more coffee and helping himself to another stem of the luscious hothouse grapes. "The fact is, I haven't found the right man to take charge of it yet. When you come to think of it, my son, the right man is a rare commodity in market now-a-days. If you had not the other department in hand so thoroughly I should be almost inclined to put you in there for a time till I could find some one else. I believe the time is ripe for such a business, but the right man has not appeared yet, and without him it would be worse than useless to attempt it."

"I wish you could get the fellow I met over in Paris. He would be just the man. A keener eye for business I

172

never saw, and I happen to know he made several
points for his house when he was over there. He was a
mighty fine fellow. I got in with him on the voyage by a
little accident that made it rather necessary for me to
give up my stateroom to a lady who was suddenly taken
ill and wanted to be next to her friends. I could not exchange with her and so I sought the only other place
left, which was to share a stateroom with Winthrop. And
he was good company, I tell you. We grew so intimate
that we took lodgings together while he stayed in Paris,
which wasn't long, so that I got to see more of him than
simply as an acquaintance."

"Winthrop, did you say?" asked Celia, turning her
bright eyes toward her brother. "Did he live in this city? I
wonder if it was my Mrs. Winthrop's husband?"

"Yes, he lived here—is confidential everything at Marshall & Sylvester's, or was when he was over. His name
is Claude Winthrop. But how would you ever know
them?"

There followed a merry laugh at Celia's expense.

"Oh, she picked them up by means of her unfortunate
habit of always rushing ahead without knowing what
she is doing," said her mother resignedly.

"Now mamma, you know you approve of Mrs. Winthrop, quite."

"Well, she is not so bad as some; I must admit, Celia,
she is quite presentable, though I don't know but it will
encourage you in your carelessness to say so, for the next
one you take up may not be."

"The next one she's taken up is a *man*, mamma," said
Marion, a fourteen-year-old girl who inherited her
mother's face and many of her tastes and qualities, and
was not easily disconcerted. "And you'd better look out
for her or she'll soon be putting on black and going as a
missionary. He's a minister this time."

"Marion!" said Celia reproachfully, her cheeks growing all too rosy for comfort.

"Well, didn't I hear you promising to go slumming
with him tomorrow? and to a meeting the next evening?
It seems to me you're getting pretty thick when you
come to think that is the night of the Grahams' theatre

party. If I was in society you wouldn't catch me running off to any college settlements if I could help it. You needn't get mad. I thought I ought to tell mamma before it was too late, and this is a good time for it when you can have the opinion of the whole family on him. I have only done it for your good."

Celia's cheeks were very red indeed now and a suspicious moisture was in her eyes, though her father and brother were laughing over her sister's pertness.

Mrs. Lyman looked searchingly at Celia. Anything extraordinary was entirely consistent with her elder daughter's character and she appreciated to the full her younger daughter's worldly common sense.

"What does she mean, Celia?" asked the mother commandingly.

"I suppose she means Mr. Carter, mamma," said Celia, almost ready to cry with vexation. She had not intended to have her plans flaunted thus before the whole family. "He is Doctor Carter's brother and he is a theological student. He has been making some sociological studies in the lower quarter of the city, in the college settlement. He walked home with me from Mrs. Winthrop's to-day when I took the flowers to her, you know, and I was very much interested in the account of his work. He asked me to go with him and the doctor to-morrow to visit the settlement house."

"No doubt!" answered the mother. "Of course you were interested. I never knew you not to be where it was a case of needed discretion. And I suppose you proposed to go down there and run the risk of bringing home the smallpox and typhoid fever and a few other pleasant diseases, did you?" She spoke sternly and Celia felt there was no hope for her plans, but she put in a protest.

"Indeed, mamma, it is perfectly safe there. The doctor goes every day, and he said it was all right."

"Yes, and I was coming in from school when they stood at the steps fixing it all out, and I saw them smiling and made up my mind somebody better keep watch out, for he has been here before, and so I just stayed in the vestibule behind the door till they——" put in the irrepressible Marion, her eyes lit by triumph that she had brought the culprit to justice. She could always depend on her mother to do the right thing.

"Marion! you may leave the room," was the unexpected command from the father, and Marion stopped suddenly with her cake half-way to her mouth.

"But papa, I——" she began with assurance.

"Leave the room! Put down that cake, and leave the room without another word," said the father sternly.

And Marion obeyed.

But the mother was bent on searching Celia through and through. She did not intend her plans for a brilliant marriage to be upset by any theological student.

"Celia, answer me," she went on, "did you really intend to go down into that awful part of the city?"

"I should like to, mamma," was the meek answer. All she wanted now was to get quietly out of the room.

"I can see no possible harm in her going down there if Doctor Carter is along," spoke up the father unexpectedly. "Let her go if she wants to. It can't hurt her."

"Mr. Lyman, do you know what you are saying?" asked his wife in horrified tones.

"I certainly do, Mrs. Lyman. I went down there myself once to see a miserable old tenement I owned. Some of their people came after me and told me what a rat-hole it was, and kept at me till I went, and the result was I had to tear it down and build it all over. It isn't a very pretty spot, but you'll certainly find it interesting, if that's what you want, Celia."

Celia looked her gratitude to her father, and her mother sat back compelled to be resigned, but not content.

"And what was this about a meeting on the night of the theatre party?" she questioned, taking new fire at thought of Marion's words.

"It was nothing but an evangelistic meeting in the Academy of Music," faltered Celia.

"And you promised to go?" demanded the mother.

"Yes, mother."

"And with a nobody of a theological student?"

Celia's gaze was on her plate where she was trying to

hide her confusion, but at this probing she roused with a flash in her eye that reminded one of her father, and answered:

"Well, mother, I didn't see any reason why I shouldn't. The doctor's wife is going too. I have seen that play a hundred times, and I'm bored to death with it anyway, and besides I can't endure Dudley Fenwick, and I know if I went I should have to, all the evening."

"And you can endure this poor theological student, can you, little sister? There's nothing like being frank. I guess I shall have to look him up."

The brother's tone was sympathetic in spite of the twinkle of fun in his eyes.

"Do," said the father. "Look him up, Howard. And meantime, mother, I think we can trust Celia not to be indiscreet. Let the child go to the meeting if she prefers, and let the matter rest until Howard gives us his verdict. There are worse people than theological students in this world, and worse places than religious meetings. It strikes me she looks a little thin these days. One theatre party less won't harm her."

"Oh, very well, if you'll answer for the consequences, Mr. Lyman," said the wife with compressed lips, and she gave the signal for leaving the table.

But Celia did not follow her mother immediately, having no desire for a long lecture which she knew would be hers. She was not prepared for her mother's searching questions. There were some things which must be answered in her own heart first before they were brought to the light of her mother's practical worldly tests, and she had not allowed herself to ask these questions as yet. So she turned aside and lingered in the library with her father and brother, and slipped a loving hand into her father's as she sat on a hassock at his feet and rested her head on the arm of his leather chair.

He laid his hand lovingly on her head in recognition of a silent bond between them and went on with his talk, while the brother, watching her, thought how pretty and graceful she was growing.

"Tell me more about this fellow Winthrop. Do you

think he could be had if we made it worth while to him?"

The young man entered into a detailed description of some business enterprises in which Claude had acted wisely and well, and the father listened, growing more interested with each new incident.

Finally he turned to Celia.

"And so you know the Winthrops, do you, daughter? Tell me all you know about them. It sometimes takes two or three witnesses to establish a fact. Are you as enthusiastic as your brother?"

Celia launched into a full description of her first conversation with Mrs. Winthrop in church, and the misplaced invitation.

Over the call that she and her mother made later upon Mrs. Winthrop the father and son laughed long and loud, and Mrs. Lyman in the parlor heard it and moved her daintily shod feet uneasily. What new folly were those two encouraging in Celia, now? she wondered.

Celia could talk well when she was interested, and she felt just now that she had her audience, so she went on to describe Mrs. Winthrop in her home, her beauty and her grace and sweetness, the evening at the Washburns', her own private opinion of her friend's successes and triumphs in society, her manner so free from all artificiality. Then her fall and illness. Here she hesitated. This had been the turning-point in her own life she now began to feel. Should she, or should she not speak of that morning and her song beside the sick-room door? With sudden resolve, glancing up quickly to see if both were interested, she dashed in. Her cheeks glowed crimson, for she was speaking of things she had not been taught to think much about, and there was a constraint about both her listeners, but their interest evidently did not flag.

She began on the doorstep that bright crisp morning when she had called to see how Mrs. Winthrop was, and Doctor Carter and his brother drove up to the door. She let them feel the hush of the sad home that had so deeply affected her. From their own knowledge of her they read between the lines how hard it had been for her to accede to the doctor's request and sing. She even told them of her glimpse of the sorrowing husband and the droning monotony of the voice that went on and on in that one dreadful sentence about the pattern.

Inadvertently each of the listeners noted how well she told what the young minister had said, and laid it up in his heart for future reference when that young man should come in for his reckoning. They did not interrupt her till she came to a sudden halt, at a loss how to explain the various walks and talks with Mr. Carter, to which she found herself confessing.

But they were kindly eyes that searched her face, as much of it as could be seen, and her father patted her gently on her head again, and she was soothed.

"Well, now I've been thinking of a plan," said the father when they had sat for several minutes in silence, "and I guess it may prove of some benefit to both them and us. I like all you say about that man. I believe he may be the man for our business. But the next thing is to get hold of him. We must work it gently. Of course if he is a fixture with Marshall & Sylvester, or bound to them by honor in any way, there will be no use in trying. But that will be to find out. He has a right to better himself if he can, and perhaps we can put him in the way of it. Now, daughter, isn't it almost time for Lent to come when you gay butterflies of fashion are allowed a little rest? What? Next week? Why, I didn't realize the winter was so nearly gone. Well, that suits admirably. Mother won't have so many plans for you, Celia, and so it won't bother her any. And by that time your invalid ought to be able to travel. They'll be sending her away I suppose for a while."

"Oh, yes," interrupted Celia eagerly, "I heard Doctor Carter tell Mr. Winthrop yesterday that if she kept on improving as she had done the last two days he would soon be able to send her off to get a breath of sea air. But I don't believe they can go anywhere for I saw his face get awfully sad when the doctor said it and he didn't answer a word, just went and stood by the window and looked out at nothing."

"Ah! excellent!" said Mr. Lyman, looking pleased. "All the better for our plans if he can't afford it. Now what I propose is this: Celia, you and Howard take one of the servants, take Jane, mother won't miss her much, you know, and run down to the shore for a couple of weeks and invite your friends to come and stay with you a little while. It can be done in such a way that they won't feel uncomfortable about accepting the invitation. Probably Mr. Winthrop may not be able to be there all the time, but he can run up and down morning and evening with Howard, and that will afford you, son, an excellent opportunity for studying him and also for bringing things to the proper point for a business proposition if we consider that wise. I will run down myself if I can, for over Sunday, and meet him. Then we can talk things over at our leisure. How would you like that?"

Celia's eyes danced with pleasure. There had not been anything so pleasant proposed to her since she left the days of doll houses and had a real fire in her cookstove with permission to cook anything she pleased for her dolls. Besides, it would give her a respite from the endless round of irksome society duties, which her mother kept her working at so constantly. She had been as eager as any girl about the gayeties of society, but when it came to the duty part, the calls and teas at the homes of stupid people about whom she cared not a row of pins, Celia was very loath to obey.

They talked so long about the new plans that Mrs. Lyman sent to know if they were coming up to the sitting room that evening at all, and reluctantly they closed the subject with a whispered word from her father to Celia that she might open the subject with the Winthrops and the doctor as soon as she saw fit.

Then the three went upstairs mutually agreed to say nothing about it that night to the mother.

Howard and his sister went at once to the piano. On the music rack lay a collection of some of the finest compositions of sacred music. Howard took it up and turning the leaves read the name "George H. Carter," written at the top. Celia saw the quick look he gave her and her cheeks burned again, but she was pleased when he laid the book open on the piano and said: "That's very fine music, all of it, little sister. I admire his taste. Let's try this one."

They sang on and Mr. Lyman and his wife sat and read. But Celia felt that something had been recognized between herself and her brother that made things more definite in herself than she had planned to have them. She wondered why it was that she was glad that Howard liked the music.

CHAPTER 24

•

Seaside and Heartside

And the eyes forget the tears they have shed,
The heart forgets its sorrow and ache;
The soul partakes the season's youth,
And the sulphurous rifts of passion and woe
Lie deep 'neath a silence pure and smooth,
Like burnt out craters healed with snow.
— *James Russell Lowell.*

To Miriam Winthrop the days now became one long,
sweet dream. Her husband came into the room and
kissed her the next morning quietly, as one would expect a husband to do the first time he had seen his wife
after a long illness. Very little passed between them save
looks, but they spoke volumes. Neither nurse nor doctor knew that that kiss was anything more to the two
they were watching than any kiss between a husband
and wife might be.

They had feared lest the excitement of her husband's
coming might be bad for her, lest his haggard face might
disturb her, and now, behold, she lay as quiet as a spring
morning under the first rays of the rising sun, and the
face of the man was changed, joy-touched, glorified.
They could not know that that look meant forgiveness
and peace for each, that the kiss meant the recognition
of all the sorrows and fears and separation—and the
healing of them.

Only a few minutes he stayed, for the doctor was still
uneasy. And they pressed each other's hands and
looked once more each into the depths of the soul of the
other and he was gone again. They complied with the

laws of the doctor and nurse, but each seemed to say to the other that it was only a little while and then they could have each other all the time.

Claude went away again in the light of his wife's smile, but their eyes seemed to promise of the trysting hour, and Miriam slept much during the day and thought as often as she waked of the dream, the dear dream, that would be hers at night when he came to sit beside her once more.

Doctor Carter told him how absolutely necessary it was that his wife should not be excited in any way nor hindered in the least from the rest and recuperation that she was undergoing.

That night, as soon as the nurse had gone from the room and her hand stole out to meet his, he whispered that she must not talk or think, but just sleep and let him sit beside her, and she pressed his hand in happy submission. She did not wish to talk or think, only to breathe in the joy of having the old pain gone. Explanations were for stronger days than these. Faith and a kiss were heaven enough for her now.

And so the days slipped into brighter ones and she grew stronger.

Claude lingered much about the nursery with the little ones and took them on long walks on bright days now. Their chatter seemed to help him fight back the depression that more and more was settling upon him.

He had told no one yet about his trouble with the firm. They did not seem surprised that he was not tied down to the office as in former days. No one had time to think. If they thought anything, they supposed he had arranged matters with a substitute so that he was not so much needed downtown. Sometimes he went out at the old morning hour and wandered aimlessly about in parts of the town that were not familiar to him, past rows and rows of little new brick houses with continuous porches that looked like an unending sleeping car, and yet with their pretty windows and white curtains presented a simple picture of home that Claude almost envied. Here lived men with very small salaries indeed, lived and were happy, and brought up their families to

be good men and women. Here might he and Miriam
have lived and been content in the first days of their
youth. But to take her here now from the more spacious
quarters, spacious in comparison with these tiny cottages of four and six rooms, seemed awful to her husband.

It must not be supposed that Claude had not gone
near his old business firm. He had mustered the courage and faced them, but they were obdurate. Mr. Sylvester had given the order and had put his own nephew
in the place to learn the business. They regretted deeply
that it was so. They missed him sorely, one member of
the firm even confided to him, but what could they do?
Sylvester was the head, after all, and he would have to
find out his own mistakes. If he thought it was worth
while to see Sylvester, he would be back from Chicago in
a few days.

Claude had no desire to face Mr. Sylvester. He knew
that anything he might say would be utterly useless.
Mrs. Sylvester had power to paint the character of even
her husband's dearest friend in colors of the blackest to
him. He adored her and she knew well how to retain
that adoration.

Day after day he tried to formulate some plan for his
future life. There was a little money put away in the
bank. Not much besides what was in Miriam's name.
That he would never touch. It occurred to him that she
must have used it for her society venture, for no bills
had come to him for anything beyond the ordinary ex-
penses of the house, and he had left her very little
money when he went abroad.

Something definite must be done before she should
get well enough to notice that he did not go to his business and begin to ask about it. But what it should be
remained from day to day more and more of a problem.
He would think until the very room swam before him
and then he would retreat to the nursery and forget for a
little while his troubles in a merry romp with the little
ones.

One or two futile attempts he made with other firms
in his line of business, but when they raised their eye-

brows on being told that he was no longer with Marshall & Sylvester and answered coldly that they had no opening at present, he would slip away feeling as ashamed as if he had been whipped.

He even ventured the thought of an attempt to borrow money and start in business for himself, in a small way, perhaps in another city or a large, growing town. But this move was too decided to be taken without consultation with Miriam, and she was in no condition to be told anything at present. Besides, where would he borrow the money if he wanted to?

Whenever the thought of telling the family of his severed relations with Marshall & Sylvester occurred to him, he would start out again on a search for something to do. He came to the point where he would have been willing to accept a very humble position indeed with a small salary just for the sake of earning something and being able to tell Miriam, when he should be allowed to talk with her freely, that he had something with which to support her.

But when he attempted to find such a position, he found also that the applicants for it were many and were skilled, and that the salary was so exceedingly small that it would be a question if they could even afford one of the little six-roomed cottages.

The fact that he had been dismissed so summarily from Marshall & Sylvester's was against him. It would have been possible, of course, for him to go to some of the friendly members of the firm and request commendatory letters, but his pride was against that. Besides, he felt that by the order of Mr. Sylvester any commendation from the firm officially had been forbidden. This had been conveyed to him by kindly hints. He felt sure that Mr. Marshall thought that the matter was merely a personal one with Mr. Sylvester, and that nothing had been said against his character in a public way. Mrs. Sylvester laid her plans well. She did not care to make anything public that could so much as breathe her name in its connection.

It is probable that the Claude of six months ago under these circumstances would have risen above circumstances, would have outcunninged Mrs. Sylvester, would have brazened his position through and secured something even better than he had had with Marshall & Sylvester. But he was not the Claude Winthrop of six months ago. He had not the fine opinion of himself that he once held. He had passed through fires, and saw yet more ahead of him to be passed through, which crushed his ambition and filled him with depression.

It was therefore like the proverbial last straw added to his burden when the doctor told him that in two weeks or three at the most he might take his wife to the sea-coast. His heart throbbed in dull aches and his eyes did not light with joy as the doctor had expected.

Miriam must go to the shore, of course, if that was what she needed to bring her back to health and strength. But where and how was it to be accomplished? What a fool he had been! That day and the next he alternately sat in depressed sadness in his library and walked the streets for some hope of a business position.

It was in one of these wild aimless walks toward evening that he passed George Carter, whose cheery bow and smile set astir thoughts of the prayer that had been uttered for him. And one phrase came back and was reiterated over and over to him, "God is able."

Was God able? Could he, would he do aught for him, when he had been all these years indifferent?

When he reached home he went again to his library where he had spent so many lonely hours lately, and in desperation flung himself upon his knees.

"O God," he cried, "show me what to do." Again and again he said the same words over. And then he knelt there silent, not knowing why he waited, but feeling that he had cast the burden at the feet of One able and willing to bear it.

Before he had risen from his knees the maid knocked at the door. Miss Lyman was in the reception room, and would like a few words with him, if convenient.

Long afterward Claude read the verse, "Before they call I will answer, and while they are yet speaking I will hear," and his thoughts reverted to that hour in his library.

Celia gave her invitation in a most charming way, as
she always did such things. She made him feel that it
would be a favor to them if he would accept. If there had
been the slightest patronage about the invitation, or if he
had suspected that they looked upon him at all as a subject for charity his pride would have induced him to de-
cline at once; but as it was he found when she had gone
that he had promised to take Miriam to the Lyman cottage by the sea just as soon as the doctor gave permission, and his heart grew light as he looked about him
and drew a long breath. That would give him time to
find something to do and know where he stood. How
blessed that would be. And he would have a chance to
talk with Miriam and feel the sweetness of her forgiveness. He was looking forward to that time as he remembered he had looked forward to his honeymoon
long ago.

After that he began seriously to meditate going back
to the little town from which he had wooed and won
Miriam, and starting in business for himself. He could at
least earn a modest income, and if there must be sacri-
fices, why, in a small town they need not be so great as
they would have to be if they stayed in the city. But this
would have to be brought before the clear lens of
Miriam's judgment by and by. In the meantime he must
do all in his power to find something better before they
went. Nevertheless, his heart was lighter than it had
been since the receipt of the company's letter.

Miriam's eyes grew bright over the prospect that was
before her, and sooner than they had dared hope she
was able to sit up and be made ready for the journey.

It was down beside the sea, in sheltered corners
where a wheeled chair found retreat and the sun kept
things warm even in March, and where the few strag-
glers on the boardwalk were like themselves absorbed in
themselves and heeded them not, that Claude and
Miriam talked it all over.

Not an experience, not a heartache did they leave
tucked away in a forgotten crevice of their hearts to
cause trouble at some future time. They confessed everything—and forgave. As rapidly as possible, but with-

out smoothing it over, Claude told all, and later answered all his wife's questions until each felt satisfied, and they had no future fear of the past.

Gently and sadly Claude told her also of that dreadful day when heaven and hell seemed contending for his soul, and as he came to the place where he had to tell of his own intention to take his life, she clutched his hand tight and bit her lips and pressed her eyelids close over her eyes until the tears were crushed beneath the lashes.

Then there were the new experiences to tell, of the day when God had spoken to each of them, and forgiven, and promised to help. They looked back into the past and saw how all might have been different if they had but followed the pattern sooner.

Claude had not told Miriam yet of his business troubles. He judged, and rightly, that she ought not to have more to bear just yet than what she must know to set her heart at rest. So he let her go on thinking that he was having a long vacation for her sake, and she murmured once how good they were not to worry him to come home all the time he was there.

It was the day that she said this that he began once more to feel the old depression stealing over him, and as he wheeled her back to the cottage he did not talk much nor answer with the light-heartedness that had been his of late. Miriam felt the shadow of his mood and grew sad herself.

But that evening Mr. Lyman came down from the city with his son, and after dinner, when Miriam was resting on the couch and Celia singing soft melodies to the accompaniment of her guitar, the three men went out to the piazza together, and walked and talked.

The murmur of the waves mingled with their voices, and Claude's thoughts were sad and troubled. How could he bear to tell Miriam the added trouble? Which while in comparison to the other trouble was nothing, was yet one which had an immediate bearing on their lives.

Mr. Lyman asked a number of keen questions, which Claude answered, his thoughts only half on the conversation, and of which he did not see the drift until suddenly he aroused to the fact that a most flattering proposition had been made to him.

He straightened up, every sense on the alert at once. His keen business instinct told him that this was a rare offer even to a man older and more experienced than himself.

They talked along and in the midst of their conversation the moon rose full and grandly over the waters, touching every ripple and furrow with a glory as of myriads of jewels. Claude wondered as he looked if it were typical of the waves of sorrow that had gone over him and Miriam, and that were to be by and by glorified into joy.

It was all settled before the chill of the early spring evening had driven them inside the house once more, and Claude went over to Miriam's couch with a lighter step than had been his for years.

"Sweetheart, I've something beautiful to tell you tomorrow," he whispered in her ear, before the others came in, and immediately Miriam's sadness was turned into joy again.

And the next day was Easter. The sea seemed to have put on an added blueness for the day and the sky matched it in clearness.

Doctor Carter had come down to the shore the night before, with his wife and baby and his brother. Perhaps it was this fact that made Celia's eyes shine brighter than usually as she waited demurely by the window for her father to be ready for church, and saw from the hotel door across the way the doctor and his brother emerging. She had hoped for this but had not dared to think much about it.

That afternoon when all the world passed by on the boardwalk to show its garments gay, as the great world of fashion had decreed—contemptible in its vanity beside the rolling majesty of the sea, that has worn its silken robes and lace of foam for age on ages, and never needs a new—Miriam and Claude sat in a sunny nook once more and talked.

He had told her all the plans and they had looked beyond the crowds that surged by them to the billows of

God's everlasting sea, and recognized something in their majesty that called them. Then hand in hand under the great traveling robe that was thrown over Miriam's lap they registered their vow to follow Jesus Christ in all their future life.

There were tints of rose and gold beginning to glow in the green of the sea, and the nook was growing chilly since the sun had left it. The boardwalk was almost deserted, for fashion had gone to the evening meal. Up the sand, walking slowly, came Celia and George Carter, walking as if every step were too precious to be hurried through, and they were talking as those talk who hold sweet converse one with another.

Miriam watched them for a few minutes and then sighed.

"Oh," said she wearily, "will they have to make the mistakes and go through the sorrow that we did, Claude?" And there was a quiver in her voice that touched his heart with an exquisite reproach.

"No, dear," he answered gently, "for they have begun 'according to the pattern.'"

CHAPTER 25

•

The Pattern Followed

True love is but a humble, low-born thing,
And hath its food served up in earthen ware;
It is a thing to walk with, hand in hand,
Through the everydayness of this work-day world,
Baring its tender feet to every roughness,
Yet letting not one heart-beat go astray.
—*James Russell Lowell.*

They did not stay in the house that had been the scene of so much sorrow and conflict. It soon had another occupant and the landlord raised the rent five dollars a month on account of Miriam's bay window, and the new occupants moved through the street under the halo of its distinction.

It was quite possible to secure a house in one of the semi-suburbs of the city with some ground about it, not too far away from the office which was to be Claude's headquarters.

Miriam rejoiced in the change and the children shouted for joy.

"There's woses, an' vi'lets, an' dandylines, an' butcherflies, an' butchercups, an' birdies," explained small Celia to her nurse.

And the other children clapped their hands over a "real live weeping willow tree" on the lawn.

"And there is a stable at the back of the lot," said Claude, his face as bright as his children's; "sometime we'll have a horse and take drives every day."

At this there was a chorus of glee from the children,

190

and so bright a smile on Miriam's face that Claude was thoughtful for some time after.

It was a lovely spring day. The air had in it that subtle fragrance that lures all who breathe to come and revel in the sunshine. There were hints of blossoms to come on every twig and bough, and the grass seemed leaping up to meet the light.

Miriam was looking wistfully out across her pretty lawn, noticing all the beauty and breathing in the sweetness. She was thinking of the days like these when she and Claude had wandered over the hillside and hunted for the first wild flowers. She was weak enough yet to long for those days back again. As she looked, a carriage drew up in front of the gate and her husband sprang out and came up the walk.

He had come to take her for a drive he said, the air would do her good, and she must hurry and get ready, for they must make the most of their first "afternoon off," as he called it.

She paused by the hat rack and reached for her hat and coat and then with sudden impulse she went on upstairs and slipped into another gown. She must not lose all her worldly wisdom just because she had greater motives to work by now, and a different pattern.

It did not take long to make herself pretty and her husband stood admiring her as she came down the hall fifteen minutes later, his face as bright and eager as a boy's. There would be always something half-boyish about Claude that was very winning, so thought his wife.

"We will go to the park," he said as he headed the horse toward the river drive, "it is just the day for the park."

It was one of those days when fashion has ordered "all out on parade." And they were there, the jingling silver-mounted ones, and the quieter rubber-tired ones, looking weary and bored in their spring array. It was a part of their day's doings, this drive, and many of them had the look as if they were taking medicine.

Miriam had not been here since the day that her heart

had been pierced. Now as they swept into the wide smooth drive and became one of the double procession that curved about the river's edge and up among the hills, she smiled to think how happy she was, and how her heart was bubbling over as light as had been her little child's, almost a year ago when she had brought her here to play.

Claude grew joyful. He felt the sweet air like new wine mounting first to his heart, then to his head. He was proud of his wife, sitting in her quiet beauty beside him. He was pleased over his business prospects, and withal there was a great, deep peace in his soul. He felt that this world of nature into which they were driving was his Father's world and he was glad to be in it.

On they drove, past the little canoes on the river; past the old pebble-dash hotels that advocated catfish and waffles for light refreshment, on their signs; past the old covered bridge, and the little rustic abiding-place of the park guards; past the spring and the grotto, into the winding drive all arched with brown branches and tender green feathery tips beginning to peep through; on till they had out-distanced most of their driving companions and were rolling along on the hard road alone, except for an occasional one who had gone farther than the rest and was turning early home again. They could look down now on the brook as it rippled along over the glistening stones below, and the little rustic bridge that crossed it, where a boy stood earnestly fishing—past them all. And now they were approaching the curve where she and Celia had climbed the bank and looked down on the world below.

Claude had been speaking, talking of the beauty of the drive and the sunlight glinting through the boughs down into the water. Then he had looked at her, but her heart had been going back over the year to the moment when she had stood up there on the bank and looked down here—where she was now, safe and happy with Claude.

But the words he was now speaking to her, were sweet and tender, and showed perfectly how he under-stood her feelings, full of a nobler, deeper love than any they had expressed before. She could not forget her thoughts and look up into his eyes which were compelling hers. And then he bent and kissed her.

It was a long, clinging kiss, and the look he gave her after it was one of tender meaning.

All softly just then there swept around the curve another driver. Her horses were finely blooded, her equipage the latest, and her silken robes were rich and fair to see. Beside her sat a man who looked at her adoringly, as she held her horses with a graceful skill, but she was not talking to him, nor did she once glance toward him, and it was not on her horses that she kept her gaze so earnestly nor yet upon the landscape, though it was passing good to see.

Miriam, her face flooded with the glory of her love and the joy of perfect harmony, looked up to see this woman, her enemy, with the eyes of hate gazing upon her.

She did not stir, nor cry out, as she might have done at another time, nor did her fair face flush the slightest perceptible rose color. Her steady eyes all clear with dews of heaven looked full upon her enemy, and knew her fight was won.

They passed as in the flash of sunlight that lit the pool below and Claude had not looked up nor recognized his friend and enemy of old. Miriam, her joy rushing over her anew as the tumult of her heart subsided, hid her glad face upon her husband's shoulder and wept tears of joy.

So they drove out from the arching branches into the late spring sunlight of the upper road that led home, and Miriam smiled to think the last shadow of her sorrow had been swept from her path, for her enemy had been met and was conquered.

When they reached home and the evening meal was over, Claude brought a Bible out and called the children round their mother.

"Miriam," he said, and his voice was constrained with feeling, "if we are going to follow the new pattern, hadn't we better begin right? I don't want the children to make the mistake we did."

And Miriam, her cup of comfort running over, assented with joyful eyes.

The little ones with wondering, reverent faces, knelt beside their mother while their father prayed his first faltering prayer in the presence of others.

Down upon her knees was Miriam, her heart filled full of praise, and upon her life a peace that passeth understanding. This was the new way and it was good—to follow the pattern, Christ Jesus, and evermore "believe on him to life everlasting."

"Oh, the little birds sang east, and the little birds sang
     west,
And I smiled to think God's greatness flowed around
     our incompleteness—
Round our restlessness, his rest."

Novels of Enduring Romance and Inspiration by

GRACE LIVINGSTON HILL

☐ 26364	THE GIRL FROM MONTANA #66	$2.75
☐ 27100	A DAILY RATE #67	$2.95
☐ 26437	THE STORY OF A WHIM #68	$2.75
☐ 26389	ACCORDING TO THE PATTERN #69	$2.75
☐ 25253	IN THE WAY #70	$2.95
☐ 26610	EXIT BETTY #71	$2.75
☐ 25573	THE WHITE LADY #72	$2.95
☐ 25733	NOT UNDER THE LAW #73	$2.95
☐ 25806	LO, MICHAEL #74	$2.95
☐ 25930	THE WITNESS #75	$2.95
☐ 26104	THE CITY OF FIRE #76	$2.95

INSPIRING BOOKS
FROM
AMERICA'S
MOST BELOVED
BESTSELLING
AUTHOR

Marjorie Holmes

☐ 25796	HOLD ME UP A LITTLE LONGER, LORD	$3.50
☐ 26428	I'VE GOT TO TALK TO SOMEBODY, GOD	$3.50
☐ 25859	LORD, LET ME LOVE	$3.95
☐ 23457	NOBODY ELSE WILL LISTEN	$2.95
☐ 26384	TO HELP YOU THROUGH THE HURTING	$3.50
☐ 25343	TWO FROM GALILEE	$3.50
☐ 26166	THREE FROM GALILEE	$3.50

Look for these books wherever Bantam Books are sold, or use this handy coupon for ordering:

Heartwarming Books of Faith and Inspiration

Buy them at your local bookstore or use this handy coupon for ordering:

BANTAM
SHOP~AT~HOME
C·A·T·A·L·O·G

Special Offer
Buy a Bantam Book
for only 50¢.

Now you can have Bantam's catalog filled with hundreds of titles plus take advantage of our unique and exciting bonus book offer. A special offer which gives you the opportunity to purchase a Bantam book for only 50¢. Here's how!

By ordering any five books at the regular price per order, you can also choose any other single book listed (up to a $5.95 value) for just 50¢. Some restrictions do apply, but for further details why not send for Bantam's catalog of titles today!

Just send us your name and address and we will send you a catalog!